The Sisters

PAPERCUTZ™

The Sisters

7. "Lucky Brat"

RIBBIT?
?
!

Story
Cazenove & William
Art and colors
William

PAPERCUTZ
New York

Thank you to Christophe (who is faster with a joke than the speed of light) and Olivier who, 10 years after the first volume appeared, are still at the top of their game.
It's a great opportunity and a pleasure working with you.
And, of course, a big bravo to the Bamboo Team who I've been working with passionately for 20 years now.
Thanks to you who's holding this book in your hands and enjoying—I hope—following Wendy's and Maureen's adventures.

To Wendy, Maureen, and their mom, Sandrine.

***Wendy:** That's bad luck!*
***Maureen:** What's bad luck?*
***Wendy:** I lost my lucky clover.*
***Maureen:** Well, I've got a daisy, if you'd like?!*
***Wendy:** Ha, ha, pff! What good's your fake flower?*
***Maureen:** Well, at least you're sure you'll have four petals!*
*So there! How lucky are you to have me as a sister? ^^*
***Wendy:** You know there's nothing worse than lying?!*
***Maureen:** But I never lie, so there!*
***Wendy:** Ha, ha, what a joke! Who do you think you can get to believe that?*
***Maureen:** It's not believaging! It's the real truth!*
***Wendy:** I KNOW! You're ready to cross your heart and hope to deny!*
***Maureen:** Well, yes, since it works.*

The Sisters #7 "Lucky Brat"
Les Sisters [The Sisters] by Cazenove and William
Originally published in French as *Les Sisters tome 13 "Kro D'la Chance!"* and *Les Sisters tome 14 "Juré, Craché, Menti!"*

Story by Cazenove and William
Art and color by William
Cover by William
Translation by Nanette McGuinness
Lettering by Wilson Ramos Jr.
Special Thanks to Catherine Loiselet

For information address:
Bamboo Édition –
116, rue des Jonchères – BP 3,
71012 CHARNAY-lès-MÂCON cedex FRANCE
bamboo@bamboo.fr – www.bamboo.fr

Papercutz books may be purchased for business or promotional use. For information on bulk purchases please contact Macmillan Corporate and Premium Sales Department at (800) 221-7945 x5442

Production – JayJay Jackson
Editorial Intern – Ingrid Rios
Editor – Jeff Whitman
Jim Salicrup
Editor-in-Chief

PB ISBN: 978-1-5458-0631-9
HC ISBN: 978-1-5458-0630-2

Printed in Turkey
January 2021

Distributed by Macmillan
First Papercutz Printing

WHEN WE WERE LITTLE, THIS NEVER FAILED...

AGAH!
AGAH BUDAH!

ARGH!... MY GRAPHIC NOVEL!
KSSS.. KSSS.. KSSS

AGRRR...
YOU! YOU'RE IN SO MUCH TROUBLE...

WEDDY, BEDAAA, BUDAAH...

WELL, IT'S NOT SUCH A BIG DEAL. I FORGIVE YOU. COME HERE!
BADAH! BUDAAH!

WEDDDYYY ...
WEDDYYYY BOUDAH... WEDDY BADEEEE...

ARGH, NO, THAT'S NOT IT. IT WAS MORE LIKE, "BEEDAH" OR EVEN "BEEDOHBEEDOH..."
WHAT WAS IT...?
YEAH, WELL, HURRY UP, YOUR SISTER'S SEEN THAT YOU WRECKED HER CELL PHONE.

CAZENOVE & WILLIAM

BUT YES, REMEMBER, WENDY...
CLAC CLAC
?!

...YOU'D GONE SHOPPING WITH MOMMY...
DO YOU HAVE SOMETHING FOR ME?
WHAT'S FOR ME?
WHAT'S FOR ME?
PFF
CALM DOWN, MAUREEN!

I BOUGHT MYSELF THESE WONDERFUL PAJAMAS.
WOOOW! THEY'RE TOO CUTE!
PLUS, THEY'RE MADE OF FLANNEL.

THEY'RE SUPER COOL AS A JEWEL ON YOU.
AS CLASSY BY NIGHT AS BY DAY... WHAT DO YOU THINK?

WILL YOU LEND THEM TO ME, HUH? WILL YOU? WILL YOU?
COME ON, SAY YES!
PRETTYPLEASE! PRETTYPLEASE! PRETTYPLEASE!
MYEAH... OOOH... IT'S OKAY...

WOoOOoOOoOo...
ME, TOO! I'LL BE CLASSY IN FLANNEL!

BUT YOU SAID IT WAS OKAY!

YES, BUT NOT IN THE MIDDLE OF THE NIGHT AND WHEN I'M ASLEEP!
YOU'RE JUST A LYINGAR!
RAGNNNN...

CAZENOVE & WILLIAM

HEY, WENDY. CAN YOU SHOW US?
SHOW YOU WHAT? MY HOMEWORK?

NO, BUT DO YOU KNOW HOW TO DO A RAIN DANCE?
A RAIN DANCE?

WELL, IT SHOULD BE A LITTLE LIKE THIS...
HEYA, HEYA, HEYA, HEYA, HEYA, HEYA, HEYA...
HEYA HEYA HEYA!
OW! AWESOME! IS IT LIKE BELLY DANCING?!

AH, NO! BELLY DANCING IS MORE LIKE THIS...?!
AND DO KNOW HOW TO SKA?

OF COURSE!
ONE STEP BEYOOOND!
AANANAA TANANAAN NAA...
YOU'RE SO SMART.

ARF! THANKS!
AND I CAN SHOW YOU IRISH OR SIRTAKI DANCING...
...IT'S A GREEK DANCE.

NOPE... NO POINT...
THE COMMERCIALS ARE OVER.
SO, SHH!
LA LA
LA LA LA LA
LA LA LA LA LI

CAZENOVE & WILLIAM

RAGGNNNWiii...
AMPF...
AMPF...
GNNNiii...
GNNN...

HEYYY... MASON, MY SISTER'S BELOVED... YOU'RE EXTRA MUSCLY. COULD YOU OPEN MY JAR OF HONEY, PRETTYPLEASE?!
...EH... UH, SURE, MAUREEN!!

SHOULDN'T TAKE ME MORE THAN A SECOND.
PFFF, IT'S TAKING A WHILE!
AHR... IT'S ON TIGHT!
RAGNNNNiii...
AGNNNN...
HAN HAN
HUMPF!
BUFF BUFF

PASS ME THAT! YOU'RE GOING TO STRAIN SOMETHING.
LET A PRO DO IT!
HAN
AAH
AFFF
ARF
ARF ARF
ARF
HEUAH

YOU JUST HAVE TO...
...IT FEELS LIKE...
GNNN...

CLOUP

AND THERE YOU GO! IT'S OPEN!
IN 10 SECONDS, YOU'RE GOING TO UNDERSTAND WHY YOU SHOULDN'T HAVE HELPED MY SISTER.

WELL, THAT WAS FUN. HERE, MAUREEN. TAKE YOUR JAR OF HONEY.
ENJOY IT!

YOU CAN KEEP IT! ANYWAY, I DON'T LIKE HONEY.
I JUST LIKE WHEN IT GOES, "CLOUP!"
?!
WHAT DID I SAY?
KSSS KSSS KSSS

CAZENOVE & WILLIAM

AND THEN, JESSICA AND HER BUDS SHOWED UP PRONTO...
JESS IS COOL!
AN IDYLLIC DAY.

HEY THERE ...!
...I INVENTED A NEW MONSTRUMENTAL GAME.
LET'S PLAY! LET'S PLAY!
IT'S CALLED MAUREEN-OPOLY.

EACH PLAYER GETS A TOTALLY CUTE TOKEN MADE OF MODELING CLAY.
...12 CARDS...
...A "TOO LUCKY" TICKET TO AVOID ROTTEN LUCK.
YOU HAVE TO ROLL A DIE.
I'LL GO FIRST!

SIX RIGHT AWAY! I CAN BUY THE TOY ROOM!
THAT'LL COST YOU A BUNDLE IF YOU LAND ON IT.

WENDY, YOU GOT A 4. YOU FALL INTO THE PINK DRAGON'S DUNGEON.
YOU'RE OUT OF POTION AND LOSE THREE TURNS.
MASON, YOU'RE FROZEN BECAUSE YOUR DIE DIDN'T ROLL ENOUGH.

SAMMIE, YOU GO BACK 20 SPACES.
AND I WON!

THAT WAS SO GREAT! I'M GOING TO MAKE LOTS MORE AND THEN I'LL BE BACK.
??

UHHHH... WHAT WAS THAT?
MY DAILY LIFE DURING VACATION!
HUMPHHH.

CAZENOVE & WILLIAM

NIGHTTIME, BEFORE GOING TO BED, WAS ALWAYS A DRAMA...
COME ON, SWEETIE. BEDTIME...
WAAAH...

GNMRK KRZZZ GNOUF
MY SISTER AND HER STUFFED ANIMALS... QUITE A SCENE.

SHE WANTED TO BRING THEM ALL UP AT THE SAME TIME...
...BUT DROPPED THEM ALONG THE WAY...

IN SHORT, WAAH WAAH AND THE WHOLE WATER WORKS.
BOUAAAH...
JELLY BEAN FELL...

THEN WE FOUND THE ULTIMATE SOLUTION...
GO TO SLEEP, MY DARLING.

...WITH A LITTLE IMAGINATION AND A SPOOL OF THREAD.
GNKRMMZZZ...

AHH, THAT'S WHY!
BWAHAHA!

HA HA HA HA
MY MOTHER AND I FIGURED IT COULD WORK FOR SCHOOL, TOO.
...SHE ALWAYS HAS TO FORGET SOMETHING.

CAZENOVE & WILLIAM

WENDY...
?!

WOOOW! YOU CLEANED UP YOUR ROOM!
I'M 'LUCINATING!
WOOW! NOTHING GETS PAST YOU!

BUT HOW'D YOU DO IT?
I CAN'T.
I'VE GOT LOTS OF COMICBOOKS, BLOCK-OS, AND STUFFED ANIMALS EVERYWHERE.

I DON'T WAIT UNTIL THE LAST MINUTE OR FIVE MINUTES BEFORE MOM COMES AND LOOKS BEFORE GETTING STARTED.
THERE YOU GO. THAT'S THE SECRET!

AND EVERY MORNING, BEFORE GETTING DRESSED, I STRAIGHTEN UP 2-3 THINGS...
... I SORT. I FOLD...
I PICK UP WHAT I'VE LEFT LYING AROUND THE DAY BEFORE...
... I CHUCK EVERYTHING THAT DOESN'T HAVE A PLACE INTO MY DRESSER.

AND IN THE EVENING, BEFORE TACKLING MY HOMEWORK...
I USE A FEATHER DUSTER IN A DIFFERENT SPOT. THAT WAY, MY ROOM'S ALWAYS SPOTLESS.

I PROMISE YOU. EVERY MORNING, SHE CLEANS UP... HER ROOM'S NO LONGER A MESS.
WHAT DO YOU THINK?

IT'S AWFUL, MAUREEN.
YOUR SISTER'S BECOME A GROWN UP!
BE STRONG!

CAZENOVE & WILLIAM

SO... ARE WE GOING IN OR NOT?
YOU BET WE'RE GOING IN!
HOTEL OF HORROR

GULP! LET'S... LET'S STICK CLOSE TOGETHER, OKAY?
DON'T FLIP OUT, LULU.

CALM DOWN, GIRLS. IT'S ALL JUST FAKE.
BOOOOOO...
HIIII
HUHAH!
HA HA

BLOUBLAAA...
YIKES!
HIII

AAAAAH...
CRASHH
GRAAAH...

AAAAAAAAAAAAH...
EXIT

WOOOOO!! THAT SCARED ME TO DEATH.
YES, HA HA... TOO BAD THE FESTIVAL'S ONLY ONCE A YEAR.
I CAN OFFER YOU THE SAME ATTRACTION, PLUS IT'S FREE.

AND YOU'RE SAYING THIS IS AS GOOD AS AT THE FESTIVAL?
TOTALLY! AS SOON AS YOU ENTER, YOU'LL BE ATTACKED, CHASED BY A BANSHEE... YOU'LL SEE.
W
CHAMBER OF DISHORROR

CAZENOVE & WILLIAM

THIS AFTERNOON, MAUREEN DECLARED IT OPEN SEASON ON FOUR-LEAF CLOVERS...
YOU'LL TELL ME IF YOU SEE ONE, WENDY?
YES, OF COURSE, MAUREEN.

OVER THERE! TO YOUR LEFT.
WHERE? WHERE?

OH, RATS! IT'S GONE!
HUH?
BUT I DIDN'T KNOW THEY COULD MOVE.
OF COURSE, THEY CAN.

YOU HAVE TO BE QUICK TO NAB ONE, YOU KNOW...
THERE'S ANOTHER... QUICK! QUICK!
OOOH... TOO BAD. IT'S GONE, TOO!

TO YOUR RIGHT!
ARE THEY RACING OR WHAT?!
CAREFUL, BEHIND YOU...
YOU MISSED IT.

HA HA HA. POOR KID. DID SHE FIND ONE IN THE END?
NO, SAMMIE!

SO NOW, SHE'S WAITING UNTIL THEY'RE ASLEEP TO TAKE THEM BY SURPRISE.

CAZENOVE & WILLIAM

WENDY, WENDY, WILL YOU COME WITH ME TO FIND SOME CLOVERS WITH FOUR LEAVES?
NOPE!
COME ON, COME ON, COME ON!

LISTEN. I JUST FINISHED GETTING READY. I'M WAITING FOR A TEXT FROM MASON.
AND I'M ABSOLUTELY NOT UP FOR DRAGGING MYSELF THROUGH THE DAMP GRASS.
TOO LAME!

WE NEVER DO ANYTHING TOGETHER LIKE WE USED TO...
WHEN WE CAPTURED PET ROCKS, OR FOLLOWED THE TRACKS OF RAINBOW ELVES IN THE SLUDGE.
DON'T BOTHER WHINING. THE ANSWER'S NO!

SCRAM! I'VE GOT OTHER THINGS TO DO.
LIKE RUNNING AFTER ME?!
GRAB

HEEEYY... GIVE ME MY PHONE RIGHT NOW!
HA HA HA
WHO'D LIKE A NICE SMARTY PHONE?

YOU'RE NOTHING BUT A PEST...

NICE JOB! RAAAH...! SO WHERE IS IT? AND MASON'S GOING TO TEXT ME...
BUT I TURNED OFF THE SOUND.
WOOOW... IT'S SO COOL THAT WE'RE DOING THINGS TOGETHER AGAIN, ISN'T IT?!

CAZENOVE & WILLIAM

YOOHOO! WENDY, EMMA, AND SAMMIE...
...ALL FOUR OF US'RE GOING TO HAVE A SNACK TOGETHER!
...IT'S SUPER COOL!

YOU WEREN'T STILL PLANNING TO GO OUT TODAY, WERE YOU, MAUREEN?
WELL, YES, WHY?
IT'S FRIDAY THE 13TH!

SO WHAT?
WELL... IT'S A DAY THAT BRINGS BAD LUCK.
EVERYONE KNOWS THAT.

"FOR EXAMPLE, YOU COULD LOSE YOUR HOMEWORK OR MISS A STEP AND FALL AND HURT YOURSELF BADLY...
PLITCH
PLITCH
SPLAOUTCH
OOUAK
"...IT'S A CURSED DAY.
BLOOONK
"AND WE KNOW WHAT WE'RE GOING TO DO...
...WE'RE GOING TO HIDE UNTIL TOMORROW."

DIBS! I'M THE QUEEN OF CLEVER AT THIS GAME.
I'M GOING TO HIDE EVEN BETTER THAN YOU!

ARE YOU STILL OKAY WITH A MOVIE AND WINDOW SHOPPING, GIRLS?
TOTALLY!
ACTUALLY, HOW MANY FRIDAY THE 13THS ARE THERE EACH YEAR?
HA HA HA
NOT AS MANY AS YOU'D LIKE, WENDY.

CAZENOVE & WILLIAM

MOMMY, CAN YOU TELL WENDY TO MAKE MY BED?
WHAT ?!

WELL, I CAN'T DO IT ALL BY MYSELF...
...I'M JUST A LITTLE KID.

I'M FLIPPERING THE PANCAKES.
I'M A BIG KID!

I CAN'T DO THE DIIIIISSHHHHHEESSSS.... WWWAAAAAA...
I'M TOO LITTLE ≥MWAH≤...

WOW! COOL! I'M GOING TO WATCH "BACK TO THE FUTURE" ALL THE WAY TO THE END WITH YOU, MY SISTER.
I'M A BIG KID!
GREAT SCOTT!

I'M JUST A LITTLE KID...
I'M A BIG KID!
I'M LITTLE!
I'M BIG!

NOW THEN, WENDY. JUST WRITE WHETHER YOU HAVE A BIG SISTER OR A LITTLE SISTER.
WELLLL... UH... IN FACT, IT DEPENDS ON THE SITUATION, SIR.
Genealogy Tree

CAZENOVE & WILLIAM

SCHTOING
SCHTOING
SCHTOING
SCHTOING
SCHTOING
SCHTOING
STOING
SCHTOING
ARGGH... I CAN'T TAKE IT ANYMORE.

SCHTOING
SCHTOING
SCHTOING
SCHTOING
SCHTOING
I'M FED UP!
I'M FREAKING OUT...
I'VE HAD AN EARFUL!

STOP THIS RACKET RIGHT AWAY! SOME OF US ARE TRYING TO STUDY NEXT DOOR!
I'M BEATING MY TRAMPOLI-MAUREENING RECORD. CAN'T YOU SEE?!
SCHTOING
SCHTOING

WELL, I'M GETTING SICK OF IT! YOU CAN JUST PLAY WITH YOUR STUFFED ANIMALS, OUR DOLLS, AND ALL YOUR STUFF THERE...
SCHTOING

SO STOP!
VLAM
WHAT A KILLJOY!
SCHPOUMF

POUET
!

FIIIZZ
POUIK
POUIK
ONK
ONK
??
OH, NO!

YOU'RE RIGHT, WENDY! IT'S REALLY BETTER LIKE THAT!
ONK
POUINK
POUET
DING
BINK
POUET
POUET
POUET
POUIK

CAZENOVE & WILLIAM

ARE YOU SURE, GIRLS? IT'S REALLY STEEP.
YUP. NOT EVEN SCARED.

AND WE'LL SETTLE THIS QUICKLY...
DON'T COME WHINING TO ME AFTERWARDS.
THERE'S NOTHING BESTERS FOR TESTING IT.

THIS WAY, WE'LL REALLY KNOW IF THIS BRINGS GOOD LUCK OR IF IT'S JUST A BUNCH OF HOOEY.
COME ON, MAUREEN. *CHARGE!*

TO INFINITY AND BEE YAWN!

WOOHOOOOOOO...

KRONK

AAAAAAAAAAAH...

BROUFF BROUFF

NOW WE KNOW IT'S LUCKY!
THE PROOF: MY FOUR-LEAF CLOVER DOESN'T HAVE A SCRATCH ON IT!
GREAT!

CAZENOVE & WILLIAM

MY TURN TO GIVE YOU AN "AIR!"
A "DARE," MAUREEN!

HMM, SO... MMM...
UHHH... MMM
ARE YOU WAITING FOR THE TURN OF THE NEXT CENTURY OR WHAT?

EXPLAIN TO YOUR MASON HOW TO KNIT A DOLL'S DRESS.
AND IF HE FALLS ASLEEP, YOU LOSE! I DOUBLE DOG DARE YOU!
I ACCEPT. EASY-PEASY.

YOU'LL EXPLAIN EVERYTHING THOROUGHLY, RIGHT?
BOYS HATE WHEN YOU TALK TO THEM ABOUT THAT.
HE'LL SNOOZE LIKE MR. BUN BUN. HA HA!
HE WON'T SHUT AN EYE. YOU'LL SEE.

HE WON'T LAST A SECOND, YOUR MASON...
THAT'S WHAT YOU THINK.
SO... WHERE'D YOU RUN OFF TO, WENDY?

I'M GOING TO EXPLAIN SOMETHING TO YOU, MASE... BUT FIRST...
SMACK
?

?!
KISSS
SMACK, KISS

...THEN YOU MAKE A STITCH HERE, THEN A REVERSE STITCH...
GAAH...
THAT'S CHEATING!

CAZENOVE & WILLIAM

WATCH MASON CAREFULLY RIGHT BEFORE HE SPEAKS TO MY SISTER...
MMMM... YUM YUM... COME HERE, MY DARLING LI'L TOMATOES.

UUHH... WENDY... I'D LIKE...UH... I... WELL... I...
YES, MASE, YOU'D LIKE WHAT?
...SEE HOW IT SCARES HIM TO DEATH?...

WELL...I ...I WAS THINKING THAT WE BOTH... WE... COULD...
... SO, IF YOU'RE WILLING, WELL... WE... BOTH COULD CATCH A MOVIE THIS WEEKEND... TOGETHER?
YES! OF COURSE, MASEY DEAR.

...BUT ONCE HE TALKS, HE FEELS MUCH BETTER!
AAAHHH... COOL!
AMPF...
SO... WHAT'RE THEY SHOWING THIS WEEK...?
... SO WITH ME, IT'S THE OPPOSITE OF MASON...
...WENDY, I'D LIKE TO TELL YOU THAT YOU LOOK LIKE MOLDY TROLL POOP TODAY.
?!

SAY WHAT?
WHAT DID YOU SAY?

DID YOU SEE HOW I WAS SCARED TO DEATH, TOO?...
BUT THAT WAS AFTER I SPOKE TO HER!
AGRR...

CAZENOVE & WILLIAM

HEE-HEE. LOOK WHAT MY SISTER SAYS ABOUT **LUIGGI.**
MUAH AH AH
HI HI
OH, YEAAHHH... LUIGGI... HER EXCHANGE STUDENT FROM MITALY?!*

HEY THERE, PESTS!

WAYAH... UH... YOU CAME BACK SUPER SOON. SUPER QUICKLY.
YUP!

IT'S BECAUSE MASON WAS MEETING ME ON OUR BRIDGE OF LOVE...
AND WE WATCHED THE SWANS... SO IN LOVE... ALL OF US.

HE'D HIDDEN A LITTLE CHEST AND HAD HUNG THE KEY AROUND HIS NECK...
...INSIDE THE CHEST, THERE WERE TWO TICKETS FOR AN IRISH DANCE PERFORMANCE SOON. SO I'M WAITING FOR HIM TO COME GET ME.

IN FACT, DON'T BOTHER HIDING TO READ MY PRIVATE DIARY.
UHHHH... WE FOUND IT LYING AROUND... AND WE WERE GOING TO PUT IT BACK.

OH! NOTHING'S A BIG DEAL AS LONG AS I'VE GOT MY BELOOOVED MASEY-WASEY...
???!

I'M TELLING YOU. YOU BETTER MAKE WENDY STAY IN LUV WITH YOU!
AT LEAST UNTIL WE FINISH READING HER PRIVATE DIARY.
?

*SEE THE SISTERS #4 FOR MORE ON LUIGGI!

CAZENOVE & WILLIAM

I'M GOING TO NEED YOUR HELP, WENDY...
DON'T TELL ME IT'S ALREADY BEEN SIX MONTHS?
YES!

OKAY! I'LL TAKE CARE OF IT...
IT'LL JUST TAKE ME A MINUTE!
GREAT!

OKAY, LITTLE MISS...
...GET DRESSED. WE'RE LEAVING.
?
WHERE TO?

YOU'VE GOT AN APPOINTMENT AT THE HAIRDRESSER'S IN AN HOUR.
WHAT?

NOT IN THIS LIFETIME!
POMPF
MISSED!
NOBODY'S GOING TO TOUCH MY CURLS, SO THERE!
LEARN TO AIM!

OOO, YOU...
...YOU'RE GOING TO SEE IF I CAN'T AIM...

HERE!
HERE!
HERE!
MUHWA-HA-HA!
MISSED AGAIN!

BRAVO, WENDY! AN EFFECTIVE PLAN.
NICE! OKAY, OPERATION WASHING GRUBBY STUFFED ANIMALS IS ON!
EVEN MR. BUN BUN IS THERE!

CAZENOVE & WILLIAM

HMM, STILL, MR. BUN BUN ALWAYS AGREES WITH WHAT I SAY...
...I GET THE LAST WORD...
...HEY, AND THAT AIN'T SMALL POTATOES.

BESIDES, HE'S SO FUNNY, CUDDLY, AND ADORABLE...
TOO SWEET!
AND I LOVE HIS SCENT.

IT'S SO COOL. HE DOES EVERYTHING I ASK HIM TO...
EVEN WHEN I DON'T ASK. HE AND I UNDERSTAND EACH OTHER VIA "TELE PARTY."
BUT HE'S BEEN THROUGH A LOT SINCE I WAS A BABY...
EATH THE ZOUP!
SCHLAF
SCHLAF
SCHLAF
AND HE NEVER SULKS, NEVER!

BUT...
...IN THE END...

I STILL PREFER YOU, MY BELOVED SISTER!
MYEAH...
...AFTER AN HOUR OF HESITATING ANYWAY.

CAZENOVE & WILLIAM

UH...LULU, **NAT**...YOU CAN STOP LOOKING...

?!!

...WENDY WASN'T ACTUALLY HIDING IN HER ROOM...

...WE WERE SO WORRIED WHEN WE DIDN'T SEE YOU.

CAZENOVE & WILLIAM

MOM, DAD. WE'LL LEAVE THE BIG ONE FOR YOU!
WE'RE WATCHING YOU!
DID YOU SEE, WENDY? THEY FLY WELL.
NOT BAD FOR A FIRST TIME.
WE'LL MAKE SHORT WORK OF IT!
SPACE OCTOPUS SALAD FOR LUNCH?

OOPS, POPS. YOU HAVE TO HIT THE WHITES OF ITS EYES...
...OTHERWISE, IT JUST TICKLES THEM, YOU SEE.
PLINF

PONF
PONF
PONF
DON'T FORGET YOU'VE GOT A WRIST LASER.
PLUS, DON'T WEAR YOURSELF OUT PULLING OUT ITS TEETH. THEY GROW RIGHT BACK.

LOOK HERE... YOU SHOULD ALWAYS TIE UP THEIR TENTACLES...
...LIKE WHEN YOU TIE YOUR RUNNING SHOES.
=PFFF=... THEY HAVEN'T LEARNED ANYTHING!
PLINF
PONF
SQUEAK
SHOOT! MY NAIL POLISH!

OKAY, WE'LL SHOW YOU AGAIN!
LISTEN THIS TIME!
OTHERWISE WE'LL BE EATING OUR SALAD AT "STARS BURGER," IF THIS CONTINUES.

OKAY, SO YOU AREN'T READY YET?
?!

BUT WE HAVEN'T HAD ENOUGH TIME...
...YOU DON'T UNDERSTAND ANYTHING ABOUT OCTOPUS BASHING.
YOU SLOW US DOWN TOO MUCH!
???

CAZENOVE & WILLIAM

RAYAAAH... I'M GOING TO ATOMIZE YOUR HIDE!
YOU'RE GOING TO TASTE MY SUPER "M" LASER!
GRIZZZ...

HEEPSSST...
HEPSST
?

HEEEY... PSSST...
HA HA, MASON. WHATCHA DOING IN THE BUSHES?
SHHHHHH...

YOU HAVE TO HELP ME FIND A PRESENT FOR WENDY'S BIRTHDAY.
EASY. GET HER SOME JEWELRY. SHE LOVES SHINY THINGS.
OR THEN MAKE HER A NICE DRAWING. SHE'S A FAN OF FART.

I THINK YOU MEAN ART...
I'M BROKE AND I'M AWFUL AT DRAWING.
OR ELSE YOU COULD WRITE HER A POEM OR INVITE HER TO GO DANCING.

I CAN'T DO POETRY.
AND I DANCE LIKE A TOASTER.
BUT ISN'T THERE ANYTHING YOU'RE EXTRA GOOD AT?

OH, YEAH!

HAPPPPY BIRTHDAY... WENDYYYY...
?

CAZENOVE & WILLIAM

HMM, HMM...
WANT A HAND?!

OH, DON'T PANIC! I WASN'T LOOKING FOR YOUR PRIVATE DIARY.
I JUST WANTED TO KNOW SOMETHING ABOUT PRINCESSES AND ALL THAT...
ASK ME. IT'LL BE EASIER.

WHEN A PRINCE GIVES HIS SWEETIE A GIFT THAT'S TOO ROTTIE...
...DO YOU THINK SHE GIVES HIM TO HER WYRMLINGS ALL WRAPPED UP IN RINGS?
HELP!
HUH? I'D DON'T GET WHAT YOU MEAN.

IT'S A MOUTHFUL, MY WORD!
IS A PRINCE ALREADY ESQUASHED BECAUSE OF A GIFT THAT'S ALL YUCKY?

NO, MAUREEN. WHEN A PRINCE GIVES HIS BELOVED SOMETHING...
...IT'S SO ROMANTIC THAT SHE MELTS WITH LOVE FOR HIM.

I GET IT!
THANKS, SISTER!

IF YOU PUT THIS ON YOUR HEAD, SHE'LL FIND YOUR TOTALLY ROTTEN GIFT TOO ROMANTIC AND SHE MIGHT EVEN MELT. THAT'S WHAT SHE TOLD ME.
UH... ARE YOU SURE ABOUT THAT, MAUREEN?
UDDERLY!

CAZENOVE & WILLIAM

OUIP OUIP
OUIP
PCHIT
PCHIT
PCHIT

OUIP OUIP
OUIP

PIERRE LAPIN
SWIP
SWIP
SWIP

PLUM
PLUM
PLUM

PONF
PONF
PONF
PONF
PONF

UHH... AAAA... AA

?!

YES ...
...THAT'S WHY WE ALWAYS DUST BEFORE CLEANING THE WINDOWS!
SWIP SWIP SWIP SWIP
SNIF! SNIF! SNIF! SNIF! ...

CAZENOVE & WILLIAM

HULA HOOP! I'M THE GENIE WHO CAME OUT OF YOUR TOMATO JUICE!
TELL ME YOUR WISHES AND I'LL GRANITE THEM!
?!

I WANT PEACE!
RIGHT AWAY!

HULA HOOP!
P'S GRANITED!

I'VE GOT HOMEWORK TO DO!
SO, GET OUT OF MY SIGHT!
EASY-PEASY!

HEEEY...
AND THERE YOU GO! GRANITED, TOO.

OKAY, SHOW ME HOW YOU GET BACK INTO YOUR "BOTTLE," YOU JUICEBOX GENIE.

HULA HOOP!
I TAKE OUT THE STRAW...
AND GO RIGHT BACK INTO THE TOMATO JUICE!
HOW ELSE?

SO, GENIE... I WANT...
...YOU TO SOLVE THIS PROBLEM FOR ME.

UHH... YOUR SISTER'S DOING YOUR MATH EXERCISE?
YES, HA HA, AND BELIEVE ME, SAMMIE...
...SHE'S NO GENIE-US!
SO, DO I DRAW A LINE OR A CIRCLE WITH A COMPASS NOW?

CAZENOVE & WILLIAM

MAKE SURE YOU DON'T CHEAT.
OF COURSE NOT.
IS IT OKAY LIKE THAT? NOT TOO TIGHT?
SUPER AWESOME!
GUITAR HERO METALLICA

LET'S GO!
WATCH CAREFULLY.

TOK

WOUHOOOWOOOWOOOOO...
ROLL ROLL ROLL ROLL

SBONK

SPLOOOSH
EEEEEH!

WELL, OKAY. YOU WERE RIGHT.

ONLY FOUR-LEAF CLOVERS ARE LUCKY.
GRUMBLL...
THE ONES WITH THREE LEAVES ARE USELESS.

CAZENOVE & WILLIAM

YOU KNOW WHAT, MAUREEN? YOU SHOULD ASK YOUR MOM AND DAD TO PLAY THE LOTTERY FOR YOU...
YUP! I'D TOTALLY WIN IT WITH MY FOUR-LEAF CLOVER.

WHAT WOULD YOU DO, LULU, IF YOU BECAME A BILLIONYUNAIRE?
I'D RIDE TO SCHOOL ON A PONY!
OH, YEAHHHH, OR ON A UNICORN.

AND I'D HAVE A VENDING MACHINE IN MY ROOM WITH CARAMEL SAND-WICHES IN IT.
I'D BUY A PAIR OF NINJA-FRARED GLASSES TO ESPY ON MY SISTER THROUGH THE WALLS OF HER ROOM. HA HA.

GREAT IDEA! YOU COULD SET UP SOME MICS TO HEAR EVERYTHING SHE SAYS. OR GET **HARRY POTTER'S** CLOAK OF INVISIBILITINESS MADE FOR YOU...

YOU COULD EVEN PAY A WHOLE TEAM OF SPIES AND THEY'D TELL YOU WHAT WENDY WAS UP TO WITH HER MASEY-WASEY.
MYEAH. I DON'T KNOW.

I'D RATHER DO IT ALL BY MYSELF, ANYWAY. IT'S MORE FUN.
THAT'S TRUE! I DIDN'T THINK OF THAT.

HEY THERE, PESTS!

YOU'RE LUCKY I LIKE ESPYING ON YOU MYSELF... OTHERWISE I'D ALREADY BE A BILLIONYUNAIRE AND I'D GO TO SCHOOL ON A PONY.
???
OR ON A UNICORN, YEP!

CAZENOVE & WILLIAM

AH, THERE YOU ARE...
...MY LI'L GOOD LUCK CHARM. I'M GOING TO NEED--

I PROMISE YOU! THIS FOUR-LEAF CLOVER STUFF IS GARBAGE, LULU!
?

IT DOESN'T BRING ANY GOOD LUCK AT ALL!
AND I FIGURED OUT WHY.
OH, YEAH, SO WHY?

THE DAY WENDY GOT A ZERO IN MATH. WELL, MY MOTHER DIDN'T EVEN SCOLD HER...
HEE HEE
HMM!
AND IT'S BECAUSE I WAS THERE!

SAME WHEN SHE ENCRASHED HERSELF WHEN SHE WAS ROLLERBLADING LIKE ON AN OLD BANANA PEEL... SHE DIDN'T GET HURT.
ALWAYS 'CUZ I WAS THERE WITH HER.

EXAMPLES LIKE THAT... I'VE GOT TONS OF POUNDS OF 'EM...
I'M SAYING HER GOOD LUCK CHARM ISN'T A CLOVER.
CRUNCH
YUM!
IT'SH ME, QUITE SHIMPLY!

!
WENDY?
WELL, WHAT'S UP?

PUUUUT ME DOWN! DON'T YOU SEE I'M IN THE MIDDLE OF EATING A SNACK?!
I'VE GOT AN ORAL EXAM IN HISTORY IN AN HOUR AND I'M NOT PREPARED.
SO YOU'LL HAVE A VESTED INTEREST IN BRINGING ME LUCK!

CAZENOVE & WILLIAM

THIS NAIL POLISH IS REALLY ADORABLE!
MASE'LL REALLY LOV--

...HEY... NOOOo!
SWIPE

MAUREEN... GIVE ME BACK MY DIARY RIGHT NOW!
IF YOU WRECK IT FOR ME, YOU'RE GOING TO GET IT... I'LL MAKE MINCEMEAT OUT OF YOU!
AH AH
GREAT! I LOVE THAT!

YOU WANT A WAR?! YOU'LL GET ONE!
I'M NOT KIDDING. I'M GOING TO PULVERIZE YOU INTO A JIGSAW PUZZLE.
PUZZLES... I LOVE 'EM!

COME ON... BUT... ≈HUFF≈... IT'S NOT... ≈PUFF≈... POSSIBLE TO BE THIS ANNOYING...
≈HUF≈... HAN... THERE'S A LIMIT TO MY PATIENCE, BRAT, ≈ARF≈...
OKAY, HERE. I DON'T WANT IT ANY LONGER.
AF AF AF

≈PUFF≈ ≈PHEW≈...
≈AHUFF≈...
≈PUFF≈
THE PEST... ≈HUFF≈...
ARF... ARF...

UHHHH... HI, WENDY...
HMM MM
≈HU≈... ≈PHEW≈...HI ≈PUFF≈... MASE...

IT'S ALL GOOD, MASON. YOU CAN TELL WENDY YOU'RE GOING TO THE MOVIES WITH SAMMIE...
...I'VE TOTALLY WORN HER OUT. SHE SHOULD SCREAM A LOT LESS LOUDLY NOW.
COOL! THANKS, MAUREEN!
HUFF HUFF
≈PHEW≈... PUFF

CAZENOVE & WILLIAM

HEY THERE, MICROBES!
?!

MASEY-WASEY, WILL YOU PLAY WITH US?
WE'RE PRINCESSES. WE NEED A SHOVEL LEER.
UH, BUT...

WE WERE GOING TO SMASH THE AWFUL DRAGON, BUT IF WE GET GREENISH BLOOD ON OUR CLOTHES...
...THE QUEEN WILL SCREAM LOUDER THAN MOMMY WHEN SHE'S ANGRY!

DO IT WITHOUT ME, GIRLS. I CAME TO INVITE WENDY TO MY BASKETBALL TEAM'S DANCE.
BUH... YOUR THING ISN'T AS MUCH FUN WITHOUT DRAGONS.
LAME!

TO A DANCE, YOU SAID?
UH... WELL... YES... YOU, YOU WANT TO?
WELL, TOTALLY! WHEN IS IT?
THIS EVENING.

YES! IT'S TOO COOL THAT YOU'RE COMING, SAMMIE!

SAMMIE ?!

ROOOH, YOU... I'M GOING TO... YOU...
YEAAHHHH! BRAVO, MASE! YOU MAKE A GREAT CHEVALIER WHO'S DEFENDING PRINCESSES. SO GREAT!
CLONK
BONK
BUT...
...WENDY... OW!
I'M... OW!
YOU SHOULDN'T... OW!

CAZENOVE & WILLIAM

MAYBE THIS ONE?!
UNLESS I PUT ON THIS BLUE ONE?
NO. IT'S TOO BLUE.
THE GREEN ONE. IT DOESN'T GO WITH EVERYTHING.

PFF!... I'VE REALLY GOT NOTHING TO WEAR.
TOTAL BAD LUCK!

HMM... I'M NOT SURE!
I'VE ALREADY WORN THE VIOLET TOP TWICE THIS MONTH.
BUT I'M SICK OF LOOKING AT THE WHITE ONE.

WENDYYYY! HURRY UP! WE'RE REALLY GOING TO GET THERE LATE!
?!
GNN...
CRACK

WELL, I GUESS I DON'T HAVE ANY CHOICE. IT'LL BE THE RED TOP ONE MORE TIME.
WENDYYY...
YESSSS... IT'S ALL RIGHT; IT'S ALL RIGHT. I'M COMING! RAAAAAAAAHHH!

HMM...
... I'M NOT SURE!

I'VE ALREADY BROUGHT MR. BUN BUN TWICE THIS MONTH...
I'M SICK OF PUDGE...
PANDY DOESN'T GO WITH EVERYTHING.
PFF. THAT'S EXTRA ROTTEN LUCK!
MAUREEEEEN... WE'RE GOING TO BE LATE!

CAZENOVE & WILLIAM

NO WAY! IT'S UNACCEPTABLE!
THE BRAT'S TAKING ADVANTAGE!

I SWEAR I HAVEN'T STOPPED TRYING TO FIT THEM IN, MOMMY...
THERE, THERE...
???

BUT IT'S HOPELESS, I'M TELLING YOU...
CALM DOWN, MAUREEN!
I'M A TOTAL KLUTZ AT MAKING MY BED!

IT'S NEVER RIGHT. THE SHEETS HANG OVER TOO MUCH ON ONE SIDE.
AND I ALWAYS PUT THE COMFORTER ON BACKWARDS.
AND MY PILLOW ALWAYS WINDS UP IN A BALL.
AMPFFF...

PLUS, WENDY JUST TELLS ME THAT IF THE BED IS BADLY MADE, YOU DON'T SLEEP WELL.
DO YOU WANT TO SLEEP IN HER BED WITH HER?

NO, NOT ME...
?
OKAY! I GOT IT!

...JUST MY STUFFED ANIMALS!
COME ON, IT'S OKAY FOR JUST ONE NIGHT...
MAKE A LITTLE ROOM FOR ME, YOU FURRY THINGS.

CAZENOVE & WILLIAM

OH, COME ON, WENDY... STOP GETTING THE WRONG IDEA...
SO, YOU SAY!

WHERE ON EARTH DID YOU GET THE IDEA THAT I WANTED TO STEAL YOUR MASON?
WELL, YOU JUST HAVE TO SEE HOW HE LOOKS AT YOU FOR STARTERS.
YOU'RE TOTALLY CRAZY!

ALL THE BOYS LIKE ME... IT ISN'T MY FAULT. BUT THAT DOESN'T MEAN THEY'RE ALL IN LOVE WITH ME.
BUT HE EVEN CALLED ME "SAMMIE," JUST NOW.

IT'S SO OBVIOUS THAT YOUR MASON IS NUTS ABOUT YOU.
I'VE GOT THE FEELING THAT I NO LONGER EXIST FOR HIM INSTEAD.

KSHiiii

!!!

YEAHHHH... HUGS...
...HUGS...
LUCKILY, MY SISTER STILL THINKS I EXIST.
HEE-HEE!

SAMMIIIIIEEE... OH, I LOVE YOU TOO, TOO MUCH!

CAZENOVE & WILLIAM

HELLO, AM I DREAMING? YOU JUST CALLED ME SAMMIE AGAIN?!
?!?
Wendy is ickypoo
My sister is gros.

COME ON, THERE'S NOTHING TO FREAK OUT ABOUT, WENDY. ANYONE CAN GET NAMES MIXED UP.
AGRRR...
YES, SAMMIE'S RIGHT, YOU KNOW.

I REALLY WONDER WHAT I'M STILL DOING HERE WITH YOU, MASE!
I SWEAR TO YOU THAT IT'S NOT WHAT YOU THINK, WENDY.

YOU WANT TO MAKE ME BUY THAT YOU'VE GOT A GOOD REASON FOR CALLING ME SAMMIE AGAIN?!
DO YOU EVEN REMEMBER I'VE GOT MY OWN NAME?

COME ON... DON'T GET OFFENDED OVER SOMETHING SO MINOR NOW, WENDY.
FINE. I'LL LISTEN TO HIM EXPLAIN HIMSELF.

IT'S JUST THAT'S A NAME I'M HEARING OVER AND OVER AT HOME RIGHT NOW.
OH, YEAH? AND WHY'S THAT?

IT'S THE NAME OF THE PUPPY MY MOTHER ADOPTED LAST WEEK.
AAH, OF COURSE... IT'S TRUE: YOU TOLD ME ABOUT THAT.
!!!

COME OOOOOON... YOU SHOULDN'T GET OFFENDED OVER SOMETHING SO MINOR NOW, SAMMIE.
HAH HA!
POOH...

CAZENOVE & WILLIAM

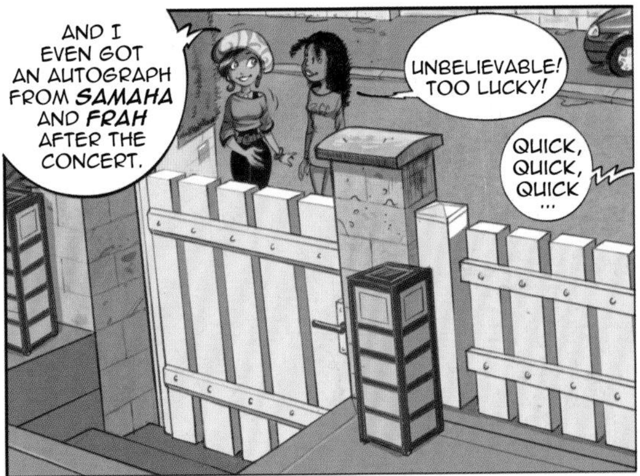
AND I EVEN GOT AN AUTOGRAPH FROM SAMAHA AND FRAH AFTER THE CONCERT.
UNBELIEVABLE! TOO LUCKY!
QUICK, QUICK, QUICK ...

?
TUNK
QUICK!
QUICK, QUICK!

NORMALLY, IN A FEW SECONDS WE'D SEE WENDY COME HURTLING THROUGH LIKE A BANSHEE, FOAMING AT THE MOUTH.
READY TO ATOMIZE HER PEST OF A SISTER.
HA HA!

AH, WELL, NO, HEY...
???
WEIRD!

HEY! WHAT'RE YOU WAITING FOR?
WENDY?!
BUT... WE THOUGHT YOU'D BE CHASING MAUREEN...

NOT AT ALL!
EVEN WHEN I RACE AFTER HER AND I'M EXTRA UPSET, SHE DOESN'T FLIP OUT LIKE THAT.

SO WHY WAS SHE SO SCARED?

SHE'S PETRIFIED OF MISSING SNACK TIME, THAT'S ALL.
THAT PIGLET'S NEVER LATE!
!!
MUAH HA HA!
YUM YUMMY!
CRUNCH
MUNCH
YUMMY
SLURP

CAZENOVE & WILLIAM

IT MAKES ME FEEL BETTER THAT YOU'RE HELPING ME PICK A GOOD OUTFIT FOR JESS'S BIRTHDAY PARTY.
WELL, IT'S NO BIG DEAL...
PLUS YOU'LL GIVE ME SOME ADVICE, RIGHT?
YES!

HELLO, MA'AM!
?

HELLO, SIR!
?

DON'T WEAR YOURSELF OUT, SAMMIE. TAKE THESE INSTEAD.
HEADPHONES? BUT WHY?

BECAUSE MY SISTER'S BIRTHDAY WAS YESTERDAY...
YES, SO?

MY GRANDPARENTS GAVE HER A STUFFED ANIMAL...
???
...SO TODAY, BELIEVE ME, THESE HEADPHONES ARE A MATTER OF MENTAL HEALTH!

SHE'S MAKING INTRODUCTIONS AND SHE'LL REPEAT THIS SENTENCE AT LEAST 1000 TIMES DURING THE DAY.
!
BEARLY CHUBS, THIS IS DIEGO, THE NEWBIE. SAY HELLO TO HIM. ROOSEVELT, THIS IS DIEGO. SAY HELLO TO HIM. MR. BUN BUN, THIS IS DIEGO, SAY HELLO TO HIM. BAMBOO, SAY HELLO TO DIEGO.

CAZENOVE & WILLIAM

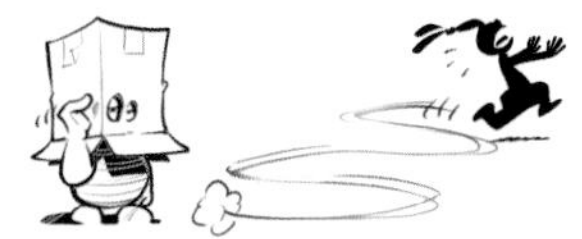

FREEEEEEEE TODAY! LIBERAAAAAATED...
I'LL NEVER LIE AGAIN, OKAY...

WATCH OUT!
TAH-DAH!

POGBA PASSES TO GRIEZMANN WHO IMMEDIATELY SHOOTS IT. MBAPPE CENTERS AND GOOOOOAL!

JUNGLE GIRL OF THE SAVANNAH ATTACKS THE GORILLA HUNTERS AND BEATS THEM UP.

BOO! HERE'S TIZOMBI, STARVING!
WATCH YOUR HIDE, LI'L STEAK!
HEY...

MWAH HA! YOU SHOULD SEE YOUR FACE, SAMMIE...

HA! HA! HA!
WENDY, YOUR SISTER'S TOTALLY BONKERS!
IT'S EVEN FREAKY!
YOU'RE THE ONE WHO ASKED ABOUT TV PROGRAMS, RIGHT?
SO, WHAT WOULD YOU LIKE? DISNEY? SOCCER? TARZAN? OR A HORROR FILM?

CAZENOVE & WILLIAM

SO THIS IS *SNUGGLY PUGGLY*...
...WHEN I CAN'T SLEEP, I SQUEEZE HIM AGAINST ME AND BOOM! FAST ASLEEP!
IT'S SOFTO-MATIC!

TROLLIE'S FOR WHEN MY TUM-TUM HURTS AFTER A GIGA-SNARF SESSION OF CARAMEL PANCAKES...
...HE MAKES ME FEEL BETTER AND AFTER THAT I DON'T HURT ANYMORE AT ALL.

I DON'T TELL ANYONE MY SECRETS; I TELL THEM TO *BIGPHONE*...
...HE GUARDS THEM FOR LIFE...

AND OF COURSE, MR. BUN BUN, MY HONEY FUNNY BUNNY...
...HE ALWAYS KNOWS WHAT I SHOULD DO. HE'S NEVER WRONG.

BUT A STUFFED ANIMAL TO HELP YOU WHEN YOU GOT A ZERO IN MATH BECAUSE YOU WANTED TO ROLLERBLADE WITH MASON INSTEAD OF STUDYING AND THAT YOU'RE AFRAID DADDY AND MOMMY WILL SCOLD YOU FOR...
... THAT I DON'T HAVE, WENDY!
OKAY! I'M DEAD MEAT.

CAZENOVE & WILLIAM

WATCH OUT! CANNONBALL!
NICE SHOT, MAUREEN!
POK

?!
CASS

AYYAAA... DADDY'S VASE...
A SOUVENIR FROM HILL VALLEY. HE LOVED THAT.
WE'LL HAVE TO LEAVE THE COUNTRY IF WE DON'T WANT TO BE SKINNED ALIVE.

OR WE COULD PLAY IT LIKE IN A POLICE SERIES...
WHAT? WE'LL GET A LAWYER?
≥PFFRR≤... OF COURSE NOT...
WE MAKE A PLAN TO PROVE WE WEREN'T THE ONES WHO BROKE IT!

YOU MEAN LIKE IN THE EPISODES OF *LT. COLUMBO?* I KNOW THEM BY HEART, LIKE THE BACK OF MY HAND! I KNOW WHAT WE HAVE TO DO!
I'LL DO IT! I'LL DO IT!
Chipie

HMM HMM. TELL ME THAT AGAIN, MAUREEN?

LT. COLUMBO BROKE YOUR VASE!
CROSS MY HEART AND HOPE TO DENY!
CRIME SCENE

CAZENOVE & WILLIAM

MY LI'L SISTER HAS A WHOLE SCHEDULE FOR HER NONSENSE...

BOOOUH!
SUNDAYS, SHE PUTS ON THE MOST HORRIBLE MASKS TO SCARE ME...

ON MONDAYS, I GET TO HAVE A BUNCH OF WEIRD OBJECTS UNDER MY COVERS.
?!
PFRRR...

ON TUESDAYS, SHE REPLACES THE SALT WITH SUGAR OR MAYONNAISE WITH DAD'S SHAVING CREAM.
PTEUHAAAH
HEE HEE HEE!

WEDNESDAY IS THE DAY FOR TRAPS.
STUCK!
HA HA HA
PLITCH

AND THURSDAYS, FRIDAYS, AND SATURDAYS, I CHASE AFTER HER TO GET MY THINGS BACK.
MUAH HA HA HA!

ANYWAY, THAT GAVE ME A GREAT IDEA!
WENDY, WHAT DO YOU THINK ABOUT GOING TO THE MOVIES SUNDAY AFTERNOON?

IT TOOK SOME TIME, BUT I FINALLY FOUND A USE FOR MY SISTER.
???
NO, WENDY WON'T BE ABLE TO. SHE'LL BE WITH SAMMIE.
MONDAY, SHE'S WITH MASON...
...TUESDAY, SHE'LL BE WITH MEG...

CAZENOVE & WILLIAM

MAAAUREEEEEEN... THE DISSSHHHHHES!

MAAUREEEEEEEEN... COME SET THE TAAAAABLE!
MAUREEEEN!

MAUREEEEN...
...YOU NEED TO WATER THE PLANTS!

HMM... HMM.
...
...
Now, watch closely!
!!!

OH, A PIKACHU CARD IN MY MATH NOTEBOOK ...
watch

WHAT? WHAT?
WHERE? WHERE?

AND THAT'S HOW RADIO WAVES WORK. YOU JUST NEED TO FIND THE RIGHT FREQUENCY.
WOW! YOU EXPLAIN THINGS SO WELL, WENDY!
YUP! I GET ALL OF IT.
wavelength
Frequency
1 Second
Time
BUT WHERE'S THAT PIKACHU CARD?

CAZENOVE & WILLIAM

...HEY, MARTY, I'M NOT YOUR ANSWERING MACHINE... WHILE YOU WERE COMPLAINING ABOUT THE CAR, JENNIFER PARKER CALLED TWICE...
HMMPH
SIGH.

HMPH...

CARL

SIGH.
M
W

HMMPH
CARL

!!!
CARL

GULP!

AND THEN, I REALIZED THAT MY SISTER WASN'T THERE...
...WELL... I REALLY MISSED HER A LOT!
UH, WELL...
IMAGINE THE NIGHTMARE, SAMMIE?

CAZENOVE & WILLIAM

BOUHOU...
...WAAAAH...
?

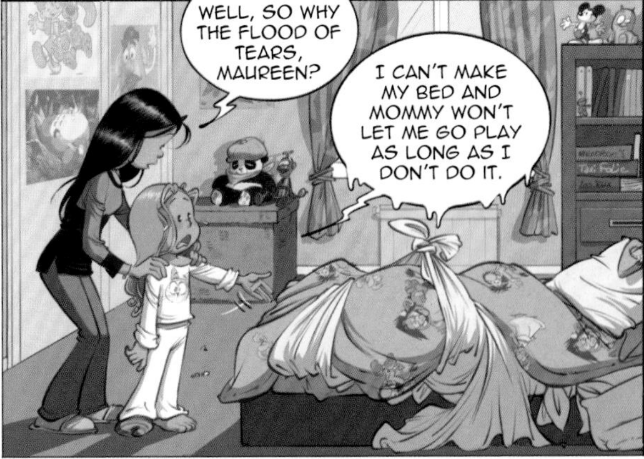

WELL, SO WHY THE FLOOD OF TEARS, MAUREEN?
I CAN'T MAKE MY BED AND MOMMY WON'T LET ME GO PLAY AS LONG AS I DON'T DO IT.

WHOA! YOU'RE RIGHT: THAT'S REALLY SERIOUS.
OKAY, COME ON. I'LL EXPLAIN AND YOU'LL DO IT.
I'M TOO LUCKY TO HAVE YOU AS A BIG SISTER!

FIRST YOU PULL HARD ON THE MATTRESS PROTECTOR...
...IF THERE ARE ANY CREASES, YOU WON'T SLEEP AS WELL. SO, PULL!
RAGNN...
ARE THERE ANY CREASES LEFT?

AND NOW YOU PUT THE COMFORTER BACK ON. THE TRICK TO GETTING NICE AND STRAIGHT...
...IS THAT THE CHARACTERS ON TOP NEED TO LINE UP WITH THE LAMP ON YOUR NIGHTSTAND.
OH, YES! THAT WAY THEY'LL SLEEP BETTER, TOO?!

IF YOU'D LIKE... ANYWAY! YOU PAT YOUR PILLOWS AND YOU'RE DONE!
PUMMELING... I KNOW HOW TO DO THAT!
SCHPONF
SCHPONF
SCHPONF

MOM... YOU CAN COME LOOOOOOK!

I DID IT UH....
I DID IT UHHH...
?!
SHTOING SHTOING
SHTOING
NO, NEVER MIND. FALSE ALARM!

CAZENOVE & WILLIAM

DARN! WHAT A PAIN. I DIDN'T BRING MY BATHING SUIT AND YOUR POOL MAKES ME REALLY WANT TO SWIM, MAUREEN.
DO YOU STILL HAVE THE SPARKLY PINK ONE WITH THE FRINGE ON IT?

OF COURSE, SISTER!
I'LL GO GET IT!
DON'T BOTHER. I KNOW THE WAY.

YOU PUT THEM IN THE DRESSER IN YOUR ROOM, NEXT TO YOUR BELTS, I BET?!
NO, NO. I'LL GET THEM, I'M TELLING YOU!

GO SIT DOWN AND DRINK YOUR SODA. GO ON. MOVE!
BUT IT'S OKAY... LET ME DO IT.

IT'S MY HOUSE AND I'M GETTING IT!
YOU'RE STRANGL--

GNNNNiiiii

WHOA !!
THAT'S WHY YOU DIDN'T WANT ME TO GO IN YOUR ROOM?

BECAUSE YOU STILL CAN'T MAKE YOUR BED. MWAH HA HA...
IT'S FINE... IT'S SUPER HARD ANYWAY!

CAZENOVE & WILLIAM

SO THAT'S WHY THERE'S SO MUCH WIND?
MUCHWIN?

YES, GIRLS. IT'S JUST THAT THERE'S A GIANT ON THE OTHER SIDE OF THE WORLD WHO'S SHAKING OUT HIS SHEETS A LITTLE TOO HARD.
TWOHAW?

WHEN THE ANGELS WASH THEMSELVES IN THE CLOUDS AND THEY LET THEIR BATHTUBS OVERFLOW, IT RAINS!

AND EVERY MORNING, TINY, LITTLE GREMLINS COME AND OPEN THE FLOWER PETALS, SO THE GARDEN'LL LOOK PRETTY.

WHEN THE TOOTH FAIRY'S OUT OF CASH, SHE LEAVES A CHOCOLATE CHIP COOKIE.
IN EXCHANGE FOR YOUR TOOTH, WENDY.

IT'S ALL YOUR FAULT!
IT'S TRUE!

WITH ALL THE LIES YOU TOLD US WHEN WE WERE LITTLE...
...YOU SHOULDN'T BE SURPRISED WE LIE TO YOU NOW!

CAZENOVE & WILLIAM

SO, MAUREEN, I'M WAITING. WHICH RIVER FLOWS THROUGH PARIS?
UHHHH... THE EIFFEL RIVER?
OR THE RIVER TOWER?
THE SEINE! PFFFF...

OKAY, LET'S MOVE TO MATH INSTEAD. IF A CHOCOLATE CHIP COOKIE COSTS $1 BUT I'VE ONLY GOT 50 CENTS... WHAT WILL THE STOREKEEPER ASK ME?
IF... I... WOULDN'T RATHER HAVE A SNICKERDOODLE INSTEAD?

ARE YOU DOING THIS ON PURPOSE?!
YOU NEED TO DO THE MATH IN YOUR HEAD!
COME ON, YOU DIVIDE A DOLLAR IN HALF...

OR ELSE, MOMMY, I COULD ASK HER TO TAKE OUT THE CHOCOLATE CHIPS?!
MAUREEN!

I'M VERY DISAPPOINTED, YOU KNOW THAT? YOU TOLD ME YOU'D STUDIED EVEN THOUGH YOU DIDN'T DO A THING!
YOU KNOW WHAT YOU ARE? A LIAR!

!!
LIAR?!
NOUN...
"...SOMEONE WHO IS IN THE HABIT OF TELLING LIES..."
?

...IT'S ALSO CALLED "PUTTING ON AN ACT..."
..."TELLING TALES..."
...OR "CHEATING...!"
MWAHAHA... THAT ONE, AT LEAST, SHE KNOWS IT BY HEART!
PFFF...

CAZENOVE & WILLIAM

PROUT!

ARE YOU BRUSHING YOUR TEETH THOROUGHLY, MAUREEN?!
YES, MOMMY!

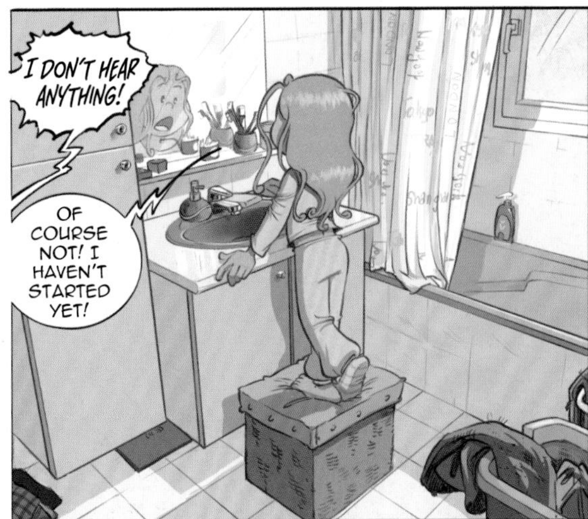
I DON'T HEAR ANYTHING!
OF COURSE NOT! I HAVEN'T STARTED YET!

HERE GOES!
TCHOUK TCHIKI
TCHOUK TCHIKI
TCHIK TCHIKI
TCHOUK

AND USE THE WASHCLOTH ON YOUR FACE!
YES, YES!
FLEUP FLEUP FLEP
FLEUP FLEP FLAP

CLEAN YOUR EARS WELL, TOO...
SKOUIC SKOUIC
SKOUIC
SKOUIC SKOUIC
SKOUIC
SKOC SKOC
ALL CLEAN, MOMMY!

AND DON'T FORGET ABOUT DOING YOUR HAIR THE WAY YOU'RE SUPPOSED TO!

BOO HOO HOO
SNIFF SNIF SNIF
?
OH, NO. WHAT'S GOING ON WITH THE LITTLE MONKEY NOW?

!
I DON'T KNOW HOW TO IMITAGE THE SOUND OF THE COMB...
...SO I HAVE TO DO MY HAIR FOR REALLLS...
SNIFF
BOOHOO... HOO HOO
HOU HOO...
SNIF
SNIF
...OW!

CAZENOVE & WILLIAM

THIS MORNING, MAUREEN LIED AGAIN...
THE WATER WAS DRY, MOMMY! THAT'S WHY MY HAIR ISN'T WET.
BUT I WASHED MY HAIR REALLY WELL.

DO YOU KNOW THAT IF YOU KEEP LYING, MISS MAUREEN, YOUR NOSE WILL GET LONG LIKE ***PINOCCHIO'S?***

OBVIOUSLY, I HAD TO DOUBLE DOWN ON THAT...
OH, THAT, YES, IT'S TRUE! WHEN I WAS YOUR AGE, MY SCHNOZZ WAS EXTRA LONG FOR THREE DAYS BECAUSE I'D LIED TO DAD.
OH, JEEPERS ...

THAT WORKED FOR A BIT...
HAS IT GROWN SINCE EARLIER?

...UNTIL SHE FOUND A TRICK...
HA HA... WHO'S THE BEST?

SO IT'S REALLY PRACTICAL FOR US.
HOW'S THAT?

WHEN SHE PUTS A SCARF ON HER NOSE, WE KNOW SHE'S ABOUT TO TELL A BIG LIE .
HAVE YOU HEARD THE LATEST?
OKAY, WELL, I SAW MASE KISSING ***MRS. GEORGETTE*** AT THE SUPERMARKET...
AND WORSE, ON THE MOUTH...
...HE SEEMED RILLY NLUV!

CAZENOVE & WILLIAM

?!
MMM
LA LA LI
MMM

HEE-HEE, I JUST BUMPED INTO THE CUTEST HERD OF UNICORNS.
IT WAS TOO SWEET!
CHOMP... ...CHOMP... ...MACH...

HMM... SWEET ISN'T THE RIGHT WORD, SAMMIE...
QUIT GRIPING, WENDY.
LITTLE GIRLS PLAYING WITH STUFFED UNICORNS. IT'S TOTALLY CUTE.
WHETHER YOU LIKE IT OR NOT!

I'M SURE THEY'D GO STRAIGHTER IF WE CUT OFF THEIR EARS.
OR THEIR HOOVES. WE'LL TRY THAT NEXT.
NOTHING'S SWEET WITH MY SISTER!

CAZENOVE & WILLIAM

ONCE UPON A TIME THERE WAS A BIG, STRONG WOODCUTTER WHO WORKED FOR THE NICE LOCAL KING...
...WHOSE ONLY DAUGHTER WAS AS BEAUTIFUL AS A FAIRY...

HER NAME WAS **ELLEN** AND SHE WAS DRAWING THE NICE FACE OF ***PRINCE CHRISTOPHER*** IN THE SAND, WHEN SUDDENLY...
Tales

WHEN DOES THE UNICORN COME IN?
WHAT UNICORN?

WELL, AREN'T THERE ANY UNICORNS IN YOUR STORY?
WELL, NO, MAUREEN... IT'S JUST A FAIRY TALE WITH A PRINCESS, A KING, A FAIRY...

BUT, BUT, IF THERE AREN'T ANY UNICORNS, IT ISN'T A REAL FAIRY TALE...
WH... WHY AREN'T THERE ANY UNICORNS?

I WANT THERE TO BE A UNICORN, WAAAAAAAHHH...
BEUHAAAAAAAA...
Tales

!!
OH! WAIT! I MISREAD. OF COURSE, THERE'S A UNICORN.

I'LL START OVER. ONCE UPON A TIME...
...THERE WAS A BIG, STRONG UNICORN THAT WORKED FOR THE NICE LOCAL UNICORN...
...WHOSE DAUGHTER WAS AS BEAUTIFUL AS A UNICORN...
Tales

CAZENOVE & WILLIAM

THIS BIKE RIDE... IT'S SO ROMANTIC, MASEY-WASEY.
YEAHHHH!
AND WE CAN FINALLY HAVE SOME PEACE AND QU--

WENDYYY... HEEY... WENDY...

A UNICORN'S LIKE A HORSE, EXCEPT WITH A HORN, RIGHT?!
YOU BOTHERED US TO ASK ME THAT?
PRETTY-PLEASE! I WANT TO KNOW!
YOU CAN HAVE YOUR SLOBBERING KISSES AFTERWARDS.

OKAY! GRUMPH! GO ON!
SO IF A UNICORN DOESN'T HAVE A HORN, WOULD WE SAY IT'S A HORSE?
YES, IF YOU'D LIKE. SO WHAT?

SO, THEN, UNICORNS WITH TWO HORNS...
ARE "BILLY-CORNS"?!

SMAK

SEE, THOSE ARE JUST GOATS...
THEY CAN'T BE UNICORNS IF THERE ISN'T A RAINBOW OVER THEM!
PFFF...
LAME!
BEEE
BEEE...
BEEEE
BEEEE...

CAZENOVE & WILLIAM

A PERFECT SHOT. IN YOUR FACE!
MY POINT! YEAAAAH!
CONGRATS, MAUREEN!

DID YOU SEE HER EXPRESSION?!
HA HA
HA HA HA
MWAH HA HEE HE HA
CRAZY!
HA HA

WHAT DO YOU THINK OF MY BLUEBERRY-CHEESE-MAYO SANDWICH?
DELISH! ALTHOUGH IT NEEDS A LITTLE HONEY.
CHOMP CHOMP MUNCH

ATTACK OF THE T-REX, "BLOZICUS!"
GROOARR
MY "CAZENOVESAURUS" IS FASTER. HA HA!

10 BRAIDS! WILL THAT DO, SIR?
PERFECTO, MA'AM!
MY UNICORN

UHHH... WHAT'S THE DEAL HERE, WENDY?
YOU EVEN MISSED THE MOVIE. WE WERE SUPPOSED TO MEET TWO HOURS AGO.
I KNOW, SAMMIE. IT'S MY FAULT!
MY MISTAKE WAS WHEN I TOLD MASON, "STAY WITH MY SISTER FOR FIVE MINUTES WHILE I FINISH DOING MY HAIR!"
FORWARD, MY UNICORN!
LET'S GO, GIDDY UP!
HEEHOOF
PFRHOOHEEE...
HEEHEEEE...

CAZENOVE & WILLIAM

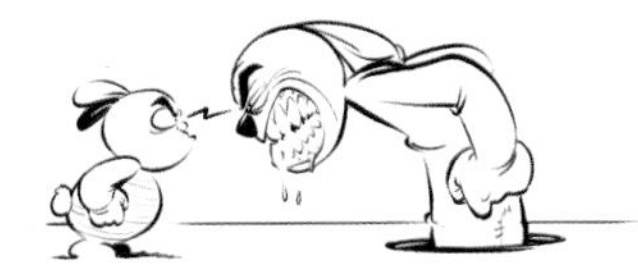

AT THE MOMENT, MY SISTER AND I ARE HAVING A "BOO" FIGHT! THE GOAL: SCARING THE STUFFING OUT OF EACH OTHER.
TCHIC
TCHIC
TCHIC
FLASH

BOOO!
ATTACK TYPE: TIZOMBI...
AAAAAAAAH...
W M
1 0

...SURPRISE À LA RABID MARMOSET...
BOOO!
W M
1 1

...MASK OF ABOMINATION...
BOOO!
HUHAH!
W M
2 1

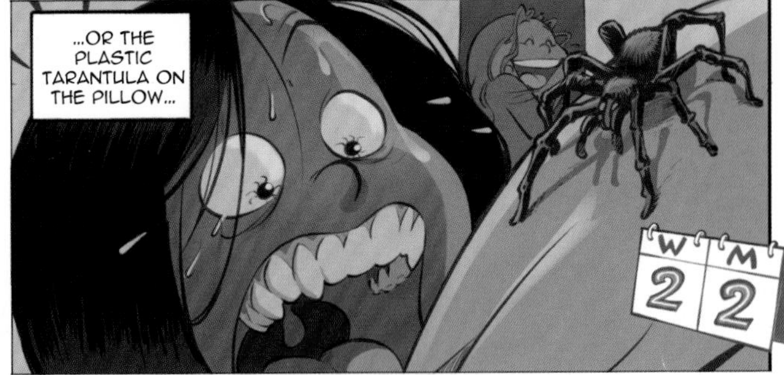
...OR THE PLASTIC TARANTULA ON THE PILLOW...
W M
2 2

...BUT I'M UNBEATABLE AT THIS GAME!
SMOOOH
?!

NOOOOO.... NOT THE SLOBBBBBERY KISS...
NAAA
SMACK
SMOOOH
SMACK
SMACK
SMOOOH
W M
3 2
GAME, SET, AND MATCH!

CAZENOVE & WILLIAM

WHAT'RE YOU LOOKING FOR, MAUREEN?
A TRAP!

SOMETIMES, MY SISTER STICKS A HAIR IN THE DOOR, SO SHE CAN TELL IF I'VE BEEN IN HER ROOM...
PHEW... THAT'S CLEVER!

SOMETIMES SHE STRETCHES A PIECE OF STRING RIGHT AT THE ENTRANCE... BUT THERE ISN'T ANYTHING THERE!
IT'S WORSE THAN A SAFE, I'D SAY!

ONE DAY SHE EVEN PUT SOME FLOUR ON THE GROUND...
...IT MAKES THE BOTTOMS OF MY SHOES ALL WHITE.
SWEEEP

BUT THERE ISN'T A TRAP TODAY?!
NO, LULU.
ALL'S WELL!
THE COAST IS CLE--

AGRRRRRR...

GRRRRRRR
UH-OH...
I FORGOT ABOUT THE GUARD DOG!

CAZENOVE & WILLIAM

WENDY TOLD ME YOU WERE RUMMAGING AROUND IN HER ROOM AGAIN?!
WHO?
ME?
TUNK
TANK

YES, YOU! ALWAYS YOU! AND STICKING YOUR JAMMY PAWS IN MY DIARY FOR A CHANGE.
I'M FED UP!

AND YOU STAYED SHUT UP IN YOUR ROOM UNTIL NOON TO READ IT IN PEACE... RIGHT, LIAR?!
YOU'RE THE "LYINGAR," SO THERE!

HEY, THAT'S ENOUGH ALREADY! STOP! IF YOU DIDN'T LEAVE YOUR ROOM THE WHOLE MORNING, MAUREEN, WHAT WERE YOU DOING?
LIKE SNIFFING THROUGH MY PRIVATE LIFE, FOR INSTANCE?!
WELLLL... IT WAS A SURPRISE FOR WENDY...
PFFF... NICE SURPRISE!

OKAY... IF YOU REALLY WANT TO KNOW...
...I DREW A REALLY PRETTY COLOR PICTURE FOR YOU...
...TOO PRETTY...

A... A... DRAWING... FOR ME?!
GULP

SOMETHING YOU'VE NEVER SEEN BEFORE IN YOUR LIFE...
I'LL GO GET IT. DON'T GO AWAY!
AND YOU CAN APOLOGIZE AFTERWARDS.
SONK

QUIIIICK, QUIIIICK... DON'T I HAVE AN OLD PICTURE LYING AROUND HERE?
NO TIME TO MAKE A NEW ONE... PFFF... QUICK...
OR WHAT IF I TEAR A PAGE OUT OF THIS COMIC-BOOK?!
QUICK! A GENIE IDEA!

CAZENOVE & WILLIAM

MAUREEN!
I'VE HAD IT WITH YOU!

I'M GETTING REALLY TIRED OF YOUR LOOKING AT MY PRIVATE DIARY...
DO YOU SEE WHAT CONDITION IT'S IN?!
IT WASN'T ME! I WASN'T EVEN THERE!
Tie em tra vole "Mashine"

I WAS PUTTING THINGS AWAY IN MY CLOSET WHEN I FOUND IT ON MY DESK, BY CHANCE.
CAN YOU EXPLAIN HOW?
PIECE OF CAKE!
TAP TAP TAP
Tie em tra vole "Mashine"

MAYBE YOU PUT IT IN A DIRTY SWEATER AND MOMMY FOUND IT IN THE WASHING MACHINE?!
?!
SHE PUT IT BACK ON YOUR DESK FOR YOU.

THIS MORNING, WITH SAMMIE, YOU PLAYED FASHION DRESS-UP... SHE MUST HAVE BEEN THE ONE WHO POKED HER NOSE INTO IT?!

OR ELSE, DARWIN FOUND IT IN WITH YOUR DIRTY SOCKS...
...HE LIKES THEIR SMELL...

IN ANY CASE, IT WASN'T ME!

I NEED TO GET BETTER WITH MY ACCUSATIONS...
WHY?
WELL... MY SISTER'S GETTING BETTER AT LYING.

CAZENOVE & WILLIAM

COME ON, MOMMY... PRETTYPLEASE... PRETTYPLEASE... PRETTYPLEASE...?

IT'S SUCH A COOL GAME! I REALLY WANT TO HAVE IT SOOOO BAD!
PRETTYPLEASE, MOMMMYYY...
STOP YOUR HISSY FIT, MAUREEN!
PRETTYPLEASE, PRETTYPLEASE!

EVEN KAYLA AND ATHENA SAID IT WAS THE SUPER BESTEST.
I PROMISE. I'LL EVEN LET YOU PLAY EVERY DAY!
SOOOO? SAY YES, OKAY?

I'LL BE HAPPY TO TALK ABOUT IT AGAIN ONCE YOU'VE TAKEN CARE OF YOUR ROOM, LITTLE MISS.
I'VE SEEN ENOUGH OF THAT SHAMBLES!

OH, OKAY, THEN. THAT'S EASY-PEASY!
I'LL DO THAT RIGHT AWAY!
HELICO RESTAU PRESTO!
GOOD! I'D LIKE THAT!

SLAM
THERE! NOW YOU CAN'T SEE THE SHAMBLES ANYMORE!
SO, THE GAME?!
I EARNED IT, RIGHT?!

CAZENOVE & WILLIAM

Hacienda

HUFF. PUFF. HUFF. WAIT UP, MAUREEN...
...I'M TAKING A BREAK HERE.
HA HA! OLD AGE'S GOTTEN YOU!

PHEW.... IT'S SO HOT! IT FEELS LIKE I MICROWAVED MY BRAIN.
WILL YOU LEND ME YOUR SOMBRERO, MISSY?!
HUH? OH, NO WAY!

IF I LET YOU USE IT, MY HEAD WILL BE IN THE SUN!
BUT YOU'RE BREAKING YOUR WORD, BRAT.
WHAT WORD?

EARLIER, WHEN I TOLD YOU I'D FORGOTTEN TO BRING MINE, YOU PROMISED YOU'D LEND IT TO ME.
OH, YES, THAT'S TRUE.
Hacienda

Hacienda
BUT I NEVER PROMISED I'D TAKE IT OFF.

OH, NO WAY. NOT THAT?!
OH, YEAH!

HEY, YOU SEE...
...MAUREEN ALWAYS KEEPS HER PROMISES.

CAZENOVE & WILLIAM

OH, COME ON. ANOTHER SODA CAN... ⇒GAAAH!⇐ ⇒TSK TSK⇐...
THAT'S THE THIRD ONE. ⇒PFFF⇐... NO WAY, MORE?...
THERE'S COLA EVERYWHERE IN NATURE!

AND WE'VE ONLY BEEN WALKING FOR AN HOUR.
DO PEOPLE TAKE THE PLANET FOR A BIG TRASH CAN OR WHAT?
ZWIPP
I DON'T HAVE AS MANY ARMS AS MR. OCTOPUS TO COLLECT IT ALL...

I DON'T KNOW ABOUT YOU, BUT I'M COMING BACK TOMORROW!
ME, TOO! I'LL KEEP GOING AS LONG AS THE WOODS NEED CLEANING UP.
THAT'S OUR MISSION!

IT'S CRAZY HOW SOME PEOPLE CAN BE SUCH SLOBS, STILL...
... REAL PIGS!
YEAH! SLOBBY PIGS!

CAZENOVE & WILLIAM

WHO WANTS A MASSAGE!
GRUMPF!
THE BEST MASSAGE IN THE WHOLE GALAXY IN THE UNIVERSE!

WELL... DON'T MAKE THAT FACE, WENDY. YOU'RE LUCKY TO HAVE A SISTER WHO OFFERS MASSAGES.
PFFF... FORGET IT, SAMMIE... SHE'S NO GOOD AT IT.
YOU'RE HARSH!

I'D LOVE TO HAVE A SISTER WHO'S SO HELPFUL, YOU KNOW...
... A VERITABLE LITTLE ANGEL!
NO NEED TO EXAGGERATE EITHER.

MY LI'L MAUREEN. THIS CHAIR'S GIVEN ME A BIT OF A BACKACHE...
I WOULDN'T TURN DOWN A GOOD MASSAGE.
PFFF...
I'M SUPER READY!

STAY THERE, SAMMIE...
AMASSAGING EVERYTHING!

FIRST I PUT ON A LITTLE CREAM THAT SMELLS SO GOOD, LIKE THIS...

... ON BOTH HANDS, EVEN.

AND... THERE!

YOU'LL SEE. YOUR CHAIR WILL BE A LOT SOFTER AFTER THIS.
!!!
YOU'RE RIGHT, SAMMIE, I WAS WAY TOO HARSH.

CAZENOVE & WILLIAM

TOTALLY LAME THAT YOU DIDN'T COME WITH ME TO THE MOVIES, WENDY. THE FILM WAS FAN-TAS-TIC!
WHAT WAS IT ABOUT, ALREADY?

SO IT WAS THE STORY OF THIS GUY...
YOU KNOW? HE'S PLAYED IN A LOT OF WHATCHMACAL-LIT MOVIES...
THE ACTOR... DOES LOTS OF SERIES, TOO...
HE'S EXTRA GREAT, ANYWAY...

BUT, WELL, IT WASN'T JUST HIM IN THE STORY, YOU SEE...
THERE WAS ALSO A GIRL...
...WHO CAME DOWN THE ROAD... NEXT TO THE MARKET... NO, IT WAS A BOOKSTORE, I THINK...

ANYWAY, THE GUY, WELL, THE BAD GUY... IT'S THE SAME GUY AS JUST NOW...
OH, NO, NOT HIM... HER...
THE GIRL FROM THE START...
YAWN
YEAH YEAH
GZHZZ#

THEN THE GUY WITH THE BEARD GRABBED A GUN... NO, FIRST A GLASS OF WATER... BUT IT WASN'T WATER...
ANYWAY, I THINK...
...IT'S TOTALLY SICK!
YAWN
SICK, YEAH!

SAY, MASON, DEAR, COULD I ASK YOU TO DO SOME-THING FOR ME?
OF COURSE, MA'AM.

SO THEN, AT THE START OF THE ELEPHANT MOVIE ABOUT THAT GUY... NO, IT WAS ABOUT THE GIRL INSTEAD...WELL, HE WENT DOWN...
OR I THINK HE CLIMBED UP... YES, HE CLIMBED UP, THAT'S RIGHT!
BUT THE THING IS, AT SOME POINT, IT GOT CRAZY...
BLA BLA BLA BLA BLA
SNORRRONZ Z Z
ALL TAKEN CARE OF, MOM...
MASE IS FINE WITH COMING EVERY EVENING.

CAZENOVE & WILLIAM

MASE IS THAT BORING? REALLY?
MORE THAN YOU CAN EVEN IMAGINE, SAMMIE!

HE'S SWEET, KIND, AND I ADORE HIM... THAT'S NOT THE PROBLEM...
BUT WHEN HE TALKS ABOUT SOMETHING...
LIKE... A FILM, A GAME, OR HIS DAY...
...I FALL ASLEEP RIGHT AWAY!

I NEVER NOTICED IT BEFORE...
IT'S KIND OF LIKE YOU GO INTO A PARALLEL WORLD WHERE TIME IS DEAD.
NOT TO MENTION THAT HE'S ALWAYS SEARCHING FOR WORDS.

YOU KNOW, MY SISTER'S THE OPPOSITE!
SHE'S ALWAYS GOING FLAT OUT...
...WHEN SHE BABBLES, CRIES, LAUGHS, ACTS CRAZY, WHATEVER.
WITH MAUREEN, IT'S IMPOSSIBLE TO BE ASLEEP....
ANYWAY, THE WORST IS THAT I DON'T KNOW WHY MASE HAS THIS EFFECT ON ME...

MAYBE IT COMES FROM HIS VOICE, OR THEN MAYBE HIS WAY OF TALKI--
?

AND ON TOP OF THAT, IT'S CONTAGIOUS... BOO-HOO-HOO-HOO...
SNIF SNIF SNIF
SNOOORRRM... ZZZZ
NNNN

CAZENOVE & WILLIAM

TAP TAP TAP

GNNN...

HUOOGH! HUOOGH!
AND-A WONS...
AND-A TWOSH...

AND-A THREESH...
BANZAI!

PHEW PHEW PHEW PHEW PHEW
VOOOOOOOWW...
I'M NOT SURE YOU DID THE RIGHT THING ASKING MY SISTER FOR AN EXTRA INVIGORATING MASSAGE...
YES, YES... I NEED TO BE WOKEN UP, I'M TELLING YOU.

CAZENOVE & WILLIAM

WELL, IT'S A REAL PITY YOUR FINGERS ARE SO TICKLISH SINCE YOU WANT TO BECOME A PROFESSIONAL MASSEUSE.

TOTALLY! WE'LL PASS ON GETTING A MASSAGE.

HOO-HOO HA! HA!

OOPS HA! HA! HA!

One Ma Zage 1 Dollrr!

CAZENOVE & WILLIAM

BOING
BOING
BOING
BOING
?

HEYYY, MOMMY! I'M GOING OVER TO PLAY AT LULU'S...
BOING
BOING
BOING

OLD MCDONALD HAD A LOUSE E-I-E-I-O. AND ON HIS FARM HE HAD AN ANT E-I-E-I-O...
?!
SULPICE ROAD
Mio
BRRRRRR
BOING
BOING
BOING

YESSSS... A UNICORN... ...HUGGGGSSS...
?
HEE-HAW
BOING
BOING
BOING

BOING
?
BOING
BOING
BOING
BOING
BOING
BOING

DADDY BLEW UP THE SWIMMING POOL... YEAAHOO...
I NEED TO CHECK SOMETHING, WENDY.

I TOLD YOU BEFORE, SAMMIE... THERE ARE NO SPRINGS IN THERE.
BOING
BOING

CAZENOVE & WILLIAM

WENDY, ARE THERE CREATURES THAT EAT WOOD?
WELL, YES. TERMITES.

AND CAN YOUR FURMITES CLIMB ONTO A STEPSTOOL?
MWARF! NOT "FURMITES," LOL: "TER-MI-TES!"
HA! HA! HA!
IT'S TINY. IT'S A BUG.

ARE THERE ANY BIGGER ONES?
YES, YOU'VE GOT THE BEAVER.
BUT I DON'T SEE THEM CLIMBING ONTO A STEP-STOOL...

THANK YOU, FANTASTIC SISTER!
MORE AND MORE WHATEVS, BLONDIE!

IT'S OKAY, MOMMY. I REMEMBER!
I'M GOING TO TELL YOU WHAT HAPPENED...

...SO IT WAS A BEAVER, THE FURMITES' BIG COUSIN...
...IT ATE A LITTLE OF THE WOOD TABLE BASE AND THE GLASS BROKE.
THERE YOU GO!

SINCE YOU LIE WITH EVERY BREATH YOU TAKE, YOU'LL BE PUNISHED THE WHOLE WEEK!

YOUR LIE WAS SUPER EXTRA LAME, WENDY!

CAZENOVE & WILLIAM

I'D CHALLENGED MY SISTER...
YOU CAN'T GO TWO HOURS IN A ROW WITHOUT LYING A SINGLE TIME, MAUREEN.
PFFF. TOO EASY-PEASY.
CLIC
NOTES

...STARTING NOW.
HEY THERE, LULU... YOU KNOW I SAW ONE OF THEM THIS MORNING, TOO, AT NAT'S...
?

HER DAD TOLD ME IT WAS A RHINOCEROS BUTTERFLY! IT HAD A HORN ON ITS NOSE, NOT ON ITS HEAD...
...OR ELSE IT WAS A UNICORN BUTTERFLY.
IT WAS BIG, LIKE A HUGE BUTTERFLY.

AND IF YOU SHOOT THE LITTLE GREEN BALL FIRSTERS, YOU GET A BIG BALL.
BUT IT'S HARDER THAN BOCCE BECAUSE THE BALLS ALL HAVE POINTS THAT ARE HIGHER THAN THE LOWER ONES...
BLA
BLA BLA BLA BLA BLA

DIDJA KNOW WHAT? I GO FASTER ON MY SCOOTER THAN A SWALLOW SPEEDING AWAY... QUICKER THAN DARWIN WHEN I'M THROWN LIKE A BALL...
AND YOU KNOW WHAT?
BLA BLA BLA
...I CAN EVEN GO OVERTAKE MY AUNTIE COCO WHEN SHE GOES JOGGING AT FULL THROTTLEDOM.

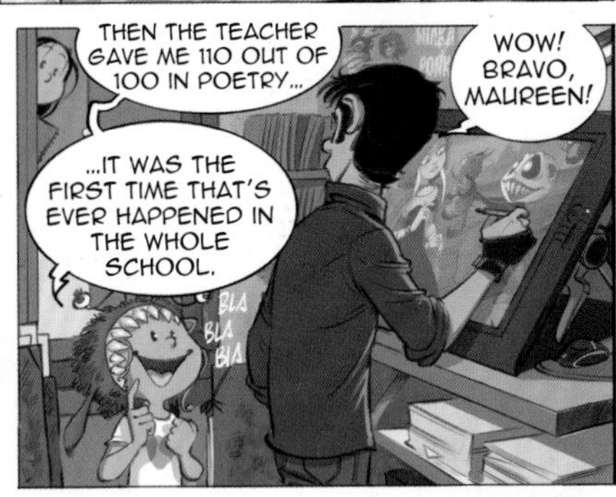

THEN THE TEACHER GAVE ME 110 OUT OF 100 IN POETRY...
WOW! BRAVO, MAUREEN!
...IT WAS THE FIRST TIME THAT'S EVER HAPPENED IN THE WHOLE SCHOOL.
BLA BLA BLA

SO, WENDY. DID SHE LIE OR NOT?
WE WANT TO KNOW!

PFFF... WELLLL... I DUNNO...
...IT'S TOUGH! I HAVEN'T CHECKED EVERYTHING YET.
...IT'S JUST THAT THE LITTLE BRAT TALKS SO FAST!
FLIP FLIP FLAP
INSECTS

CAZENOVE & WILLIAM

HEY, WENDY THE PEST... IT'S SIX ON THE DOT AND YOU'RE EVEN UGLIER THAN THIS MORNING AND YOUR MOUTH SMELLS LIKE MOLDY MOZZARELLA.
HA HA

OH, YOU... THIS TIME, I'M GOING TO TEAR YOU APART AND SELL YOU FOR PARTS...
HA HA HA. YOU CAN'T EVEN DO THAT... HUH...

SAFE! REWIND TIME BACK ONE MINUTE.
HOP

IT'S SIX ON THE DOT, WENDY. YOU'RE TOO PRETTY AND YOUR BREATH IS SWEETER THAN CARAMEL ICE CREAM.
ARGH... IT'S STARTING AGAIN!

THIS BUSINESS WITH THE TIME MACHINE WORKS FOR BABIES LIKE YOU, BUT I'VE HAD IT UP TO HERE WITH IT!

HELLO! MY TIME MACHINE WORKS FOR REALS, SO THERE!
GRRR GRRRR GRRRR

WENDY... WHAT'S GOING ON WITH THIS PHONE BILL?

WHERE DO I PUSH TO GO BACK TO YESTERDAY BEFORE I CALLED MASON AND TALKED FOR 3 HOURS?
TURN THE PAPER ARROW THERE, THEN PULL THE ELASTIC AT THE BOTTOM.
WENDY!

CAZENOVE & WILLIAM

SO?
PIECE OF CAKE, EH?
UH... WHAT'S THAT?
WE DON'T UNDERSTAND ANYTHING, MAUREEN.

ARE YOU BEING THIS LAME ON PURPOSE?!
YOU CAN DO MORE THAN JUST DRAW, YOU KNOW!
YUP! YOUR THINGIE'S CONFUSING.

MAKE IT FOR US IN CLAYDOUGH. THAT'LL HELP US...

PLANNED AHEAD! SO HERE YOU GO!
MWAH-HA... I'D SAY A PILE OF TROLL POO.
MIME IT FOR US THEN.

OKAY! BESIDES, I'M SUPER GOOD AT MIMAGE!
YOU'LL GET IT THIS WAY, FOR SURE!
HOP HOP
HUMMHUH
OOPS!
SWIIIP
BONK
OW!

A UNICORN!
YESSSS... THAT'S IIIT.

CAZENOVE & WILLIAM

WOW! YOUR MUSHROOM FAIRY'S TOO GREAT, WENDY!
THANKS, MAUREEN.
WILL YOU GIVE IT TO ME, PRETTYPLEASE?!

SURE.
IT MAKES ME HAPPY YOU LIKE MY DRAWINGS.
AND THAT UNICORN... IT LOOKS LIKE IT'S ABOUT TO JUMP OFF THE PAGE!
CAN I GIVE IT TO LULU? OTHERWISE SHE'S GOING TO BE GREENER THAN A GRASSHOPPER...

OKAY! AND I'LL MAKE A DRAWING FOR NAT. THAT WAY, NO GREEN EYES AND NO GRASSHOPPERS!
YOU KNOW HOW TO DRAW A DRAGON?
EASY!

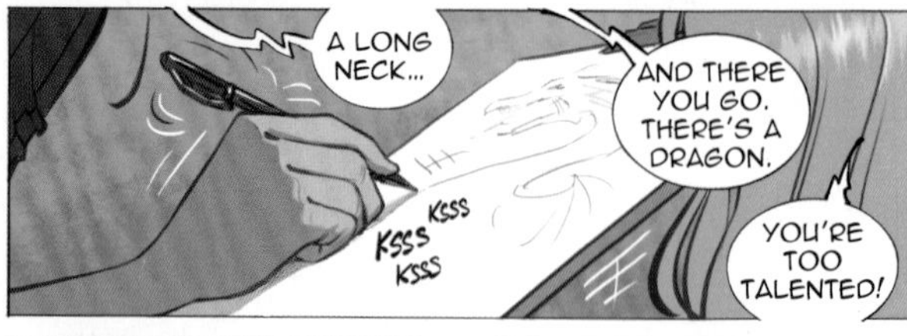
A LONG NECK...
KSSS KSSS KSSS
AND THERE YOU GO. THERE'S A DRAGON.
YOU'RE TOO TALENTED!

NAT AND LULU'LL A-DORE-IT!

OH, HEY... GIRLS...
I HAVE THREE NEW ONES!
?!!!
DRAWER WINGS CHEEP $1
TOO KUTE!
$1
KASH

CAZENOVE & WILLIAM

TWO FOURS!

ONE, TWO, THREE, FOUR, EIGHT, TEN, AND I GO AGAIN!
?
YOU LOSE A TURN WHEN I GET A PEAR.
POC POC
POC POC

AND PRESTO! A CHANCE CARD.
YOU BECOME WEAK ZOMBIES...
...YOU EACH OWE ME 10,000 BONES!

I ADVANCE TO THE TIZOMBI TOMB AND YOU HAVE TO CROSS MY LAND.
SO YOU LOSE YOUR BRAIN FOR FIVE TURNS AND I PLAY AGAIN.

DOUBLE THREES! **MARGOTIK** AND **TEKATE** ARE MINE, SO YOU PAY ME 20 RAVEN SKULLS.
AND THE "GRAVEYARD BANK" PAYS ME BACK MY DATES.

???

MAUREEN CHANGES THE RULES EVERY TIME YOU PLAY AND YOU DON'T SAY ANYTHING?
NO NEED.
NO!

BECAUSE EVEN WHEN SHE CHEATS, SHE STILL WINDS UP LOSING.
GRUMBLLL...
THE LITTLE MISS IS THE LAMEST OF LAME AT "ZOMBIEPOLY"!
PFFF...
THIS GAME'S ROTTEN!

CAZENOVE & WILLIAM

RAAAH...
PONK

AGRRRR...
I'M FEDDEST OF FEDDED UP!

HUMPF!
BROK BROK
TOO UNFAIR!

GNIIIIIAH
CASS

I'M TOTALLY SICKLINESS OF IT!
ENOUGH!

HELLOOOO... WHAT LAME GNAT BIT YOU AGAIN?
WHAT'RE YOU DOING THERE!

WELL, MY TEACHER PUT ME IN THE CORNER BECAUSE SHE THOUGHT I'D COPIED FROM LULU AND THAT I--

!!
...I...

I...I THINK I'M GOING TO LET OFF STEAM IN MY ROOM INSTEAD... HMM, HMM.
GRRRRR
SORRY, SISTER... GULP!

CAZENOVE & WILLIAM

WENDY, IS IT TRUE THAT UNICORNS EAT PIECES OF RAINBOWS THAT FALL DURING THE NIGHT?
UHMMM... WELLLL...

LULU TOLD ME UNICORNS SLEEP ON BIG, SOFT, FLUFFY VANILLA-SCENTED CLOUDS...
...DO YOU THINK THAT'S THE REAL TRUTH?
AH, HMM... IT'S... WELLL...
CROC

IF A UNICORN IS A LYINGAR, DOES ITS HORN GET LONGER LIKE PINOCCHIO'S NOSE?
HMM ...?

AND IF IT LOSES ITS BABY HORN, DOES THE TOOTH FAIRY LEAVE A COIN UNDER ITS PILLOW?
UHH...
...

DO UNICORNS SAY, "COOKIES" OR "BISCUITS?"

DID YOU WRITE THAT, WENDY?
WELL, YES!

YOU WANT TO TAKE A COURSE ABOUT... "UNICORNS?"
WELL, YEAH, SAMMIE...
...I HAVE TOO MANY GAPS IN WHAT I KNOW ABOUT THEM FOR A BIG SISTER...
WRITE THE NAME OF ELECTIVES YOU'D LIKE!
Courses On Unicorns! Wendy M.
I SAW GOD.
TWO-HOUR RECESS Thomas D.
More recess
TEACHERS LOUNGE
EXI
Strike on the 12th.

CAZENOVE & WILLIAM

MAUREEN, NAT.... YOU'LL NEVER BELIEVE WHAT I SAW IN THE WOODS WITH MASE...
...IT WAS HUUUUGE!
??
A DINOSAUR ON A SKATE-BOARD?!

BETTER THAN THAT! I SAW... A UNICORN!
YUP! ALL LOVELY WITH ITS RAINBOW MANE.
A UNICORN?!

WE HAVE TO HURRY BEFORE IT GOES BACK TO ITS MAGIC WATERFALL.

I'VE GOT SOME CANDY IN MY POCKET. DO YOU THINK IT'LL EAT IT FROM MY HAND?

UH...WAIT, NAT! MY SISTER'S PLAYING A JOKE ON US, I'M SURE!
LIKE AN APRIL FOOLS JOKE, YOU KNOW?!
PLAF

YOU'RE NOT TELLING US A LYINGAGE SO YOU AND YOUR MASEY CAN HAVE SOME QUIET FOR YOUR SLOBBERY KISSES, ARE YOU?
OF COURSE NOT!
SHAKE A LEG! YOU'RE GOING TO MISS A UNICORN... A UNICORN!

HEE-HEE! AND THERE YOU GO! WE'LL HAVE PEACE AND QUIET FOR THE WHOLE MORNING AT LEAST.

WOOW! A UNICORN...
I'VE NEVER SEEN ONE, EITHER!
WAIT FOR ME, GIRLS...

CAZENOVE & WILLIAM

KOF COUGH COUGH KOF KOF COUGH KOF COUGH COUGH
POOR KID...

UGH. ... I TOLD THE LITTLE PEST SHE'D CATCH COLD FROM WALKING AROUND BAREFOOT IN THE WET GRASS...
COUGH
COUGH KOFF
... BUT SHE'S AS STUBBORN AS A MULE.

KOFF KOFF COUGH COUGH COUGH
I'LL BE BACK, SAMMIE...
...I'LL JUST BE GONE FOR TWO MINUTES.

TSSSK... YOU'RE JUST BEING A GROUCH, WENDY...
...BUT ACTUALLY, YOU'VE GOT A BRILLIANT SISTER!

SINCE YOUR LITTLE SISTER IS SICK, YOU RUSH TO TAKE CARE OF HER.
COUGH COUGH
TOO CUTE. I LOVE IT!

HUH? WHAT WERE YOU SAYING, SAMMIE? I DIDN'T HEAR YOU.
I WAS SAYING THAT...

...
KOFF COUGH COUGH
I WAS BUSY SEALING OFF MAUREEN'S DOOR.
SO SHE WON'T COME AND CONTAMINATE MY ROOM WITH HER DIRTY GERMS.

CAZENOVE & WILLIAM

HU... HMM... AHH...
...ATCHOOOOO!
!
YIKES! THAT DOESN'T SOUND ANY BETTER!

WENDY, COULD YOU ZDAY WITH ME FOR WHILE? -SNIRRFL-... HEY, COME ON, BRETTYBLEAZE?
UHH, AH, WELL, NO, I'M MEETING MASE AT THE SKATEPARK... SORRY, LI'L SISTER.

OKAY, I'M LATE. CATCH YOU LATER, SICK KID.
ZO, THIZ AFTER-NOON?!
I'B BORED!

NOT THEN, EITHER!
I'M GOING TO HELP SAMMIE PICK OUT SOME NEW SWEATERS.
AND THEN I'M GOING TO A MOVIE RIGHT AFTER WITH EMMA.
GRUMBL... PEUH! SNIRRFL...

ALRIGHT...
...YOU DON'T LEAVE BE ANY CHOIZ!
???

BIG HUG!
HUH!

YOU'RE ZOOO NIZE TO DROB YOUR WHOLE DAYZ BLAN TO ZDAY WID BE THE WHOLE AFTERNOON...
HM... ATCHOOO!
AATCHAAA!
BLESS YOU!

CAZENOVE & WILLIAM

ATCHOO...
GOOD NIGHT... VISITOR FROM THE FUTURE!
?!

NO! WAIT, DOC! THE BUMP, THE BUMP ON YOUR HEAD. I KNOW HOW YOU GOT IT...
?

GRUMBLL...
...YOU TOLD ME YOU WERE STANDING ON YOUR TOILET TO HANG UP A CLOCK...
???

RATCHAAAOUM
...YOU FELL AND YOUR HEAD HIT THE SINK...

AND WHEN YOU WERE GETTING UP, YOU GOT THE IDEA OF BUILDING A FLUX CAPACITOR TO MAKE TIME TRAVEL POSSIBLE...
???

GADZOOKS!
UHHH... WENDY, WHAT'S YOUR SISTER'S PROBLEM?

SNIRFL
OH... THAT?! THIS MORNING I TOLD HER I COULD HEAR HER SNEEZE ALL THE WAY DOWN HERE...
...SINCE THEN, SHE'S BEEN CHECKING!
HEEHEEHEE
MWARF ARF ARF

CAZENOVE & WILLIAM

ABRACASHOO! BUZZ OFF! GO ON NOW!
HI, GIRLS!
SHOO! SHOO! GO! SCRAM!

BOOO! OUT OF HERE!
UH.... WHAT'S YOUR SISTER'S PROBLEM THIS TIME?
OH, THAT?

I TOLD HER SHE PROBABLY CAUGHT HER GERMS PLAYING IN THE GARDEN.
GET OUT OF HERE! NOW!
I NEVER WANT TO SEE YOU ANYMORE!

GO BACK HOME!
SHE'S BEEN TRYING TO GET THEM TO GO EVER SINCE.
HA HAHA!
MWAH
HEE HEE-HEE HEE
HEE HEE
CAZENOVE & WILLIAM

SUPER-SPEED...
...GOT IT!
BEBEEEP!
VVVVVVVVNVR.OOO OOOOAAR...

SUPER STRENGTH...
...CHECK!
GRRRAAA...
SUPER ARMS OF IRON
wendy 10
hulk 0
BROCK

FINGERTIP LASER...
...YEP!
OWWWW...
SHABAM

ABLE TO SEE THROUGH WALLS...
BRUSH BRUSH BRUSH
STILL THERE...

FLY LIKE A BIRD...
...I CAN DO THAT, TOO!

IT'S ALL GOOD, SISTER. WE'VE GONE THROUGH OUR SUPER POWERS.
YES, WE'VE REALLY GOT A WHOLE BUNCH OF THEM!

BUT THE POWER TO CLEAN UP OUR ROOMS BEFORE WATCHING TV...
...THAT, WE DON'T HAVE!
A POWER LIKE THAT MEANS TOO MUCH WORK!

CAZENOVE & WILLIAM

YOOHOO! I WON THE TOUR DE FRANCE!
MAUREEN: 1 DADDY: ZERO!
AR... HUFF PUFF

COME ON, COME ON! DON'T JUST STAND THERE ALL WORN OUT, DADDY...
NOW WE HAVE TO WIN THE WORLD CUP IN SOCCER.

IT'S TOO COOL OF YOU TO HELP ME CLEAN MY ROOM, MOM.
HERE! ONLY THREE STACKS OF SWEATERS ARE LEFT.

PUT THEM ON THE DRESSER THERE.
MOVE THE BED TO THE CORNER...
THE SHOE TREE IN THE BACK...
AND THEN WE'LL PUT UP THE NEW SHELVES...

YES, YES, WE KNOW, WE KNOW...
WE'LL BRUSH OUR TEETH THOROUGHLY ...
A SHOWER AND THEN TO BED!

SO?
IT'S GOOD.

ZZ SNORRR SNNN ZZ ZZ
OPERATION "WEAR OUT THE PARENTS" WAS A SUCCESS, SISTER.
YES! WE WON'T MISS OUR EPISODE OF "SPACE ZOMBIES..."
...JUST BECAUSE IT'S TOO LATE.
ZAP

CAZENOVE & WILLIAM

AND SAMAHA AND FRAH WERE THERE SINGING IN THE SEATS...
...NOT EVEN SIX FEET AWAY FROM US...
THAT GROUP IS TOO AWESOME!

SAY, MISS PINOCCHIO, WEREN'T YOU SUPPOSED TO FINISH YOUR HOMEWORK THIS AFTERNOON?!
WELLLLL... UHHHHH...

INSTEAD, YOU WENT CRAZY WITH NAT AND LULU, I BET?!
IT'S NOT MY FAULT. I LOVE ROLLERBLADING.

OKAY. BUT YOU LIED AGAIN AND YOU KNOW OUR PARENTS DON'T LIKE THAT AT ALL.
I GUESS THERE'S ONLY ONE THING LEFT TO DO...
HEY
?!

MERCY, WENDY... DON'T SAY ANYTHING!
I...I'LL GIVE YOU ALL MY EASTER EGGS, EVEN THE CARAMEL ONES...
I'LL EVEN PUT MY FOUR-LEAF CLOVER ON YOUR PILLOW EVERY MORNING...
...MY NICEST STUFFED ANIMALS...
...MY COMICS ...
...MY NINTENDOX...
... DON'T SAY ANYTHING, PRETTYPLEASE PRETTYPLEASE PRETTYPLEASE...

WENDY, DID YOU REALLY MEAN TO BLACKMAIL YOUR SISTER JUST NOW?

OF COURSE NOT, SAMMIE...
...I JUST WANTED TO TEACH HER TO LIE WITHOUT GETTING CAUGHT.
YUM YUM CRUNCH
BUT THIS ISN'T SO BAD, ALL THINGS CONSIDERED, HA HA!
HERE! HAVE ANOTHER CHOCOLATE.
PAQUES

CAZENOVE & WILLIAM

OKAY, MAUREEN, YOU'RE GOING TO TOSS ME THAT BALL, RIGHT?
COME ONNNN... NOW'S NOT THE TIME TO ADMIRE THE STREET...
TEET TEET TEET
FSHH
BRRRR

BUT LOOK AT THIS CRUDDY PIECE OF PAPER IN THE TOTALLY CLEAN STREET...
...ULTRA GROSS!

POOH! AND THIS OLD BANANA PEEL...
YUCK!
... LEFT ON MRS. GEORGETTE'S TOTALLY COOL WALL.

AYYAHHH! IT'S A CON-SPEAR-RACING OR WHAT?!
THESE STAIRS ARE WORSE THAN A DUMP YARD!

TOSS IT ALL INTO THE GARBAGE CAN SO WE CAN FINALLY START PLAYING.
YES, YES. THERE! THERE!

BUT... BUT...
OOOH, NOOOO...

I CAN'T TOSS AAAAANY-THING...
THE GARBAGE CANS ARE TOO CLEAN...
PSHEEE

CAZENOVE & WILLIAM

AMPFF...
IS SOMETHING WRONG, MAUREEN? DID YOU LOSE YOUR MR. BUN BUN?!
UH, OH...

WORSE, LULU! MY SISTER IS DOING A MAJOR ROOM CLEAN-UP.
AH... THAT'S TOTALLY UNCOOL!

AND SO YOU'RE GOING TO HAVE DO THE SAME THING TO YOURS?
THAT'S NOT GOOD, RIGHT?!

THAT MEANS SHE'LL BE DOING SORTAGE AND LOTS OF TIDYAGE OF HER THINGS AND ALL...
OH, YEAH... THAT'S A BUMMER, HUMMER.

YOU'RE GOING TO HAVE TO HELP HER THROW THINGS AWAY OR CARRY THEM IN BOXES... LOTS OF HEAVY THINGS?
BUT, OH... COME ON, LULU...
DID YOU LEAVE YOUR BRAIN IN THE DRAIN ALL NIGHT OR WHAT?!

GET A LOAD OF THAT!
HOW'M I SUPPOSED TO GET MY BEARINGS WHEN I RUMMAGE THROUGH HER THINGS IF SHE WON'T STOP MOVING EVERYTHING AROUND ALL THE TIME?
SHKRK

CAZENOVE & WILLIAM

MMM... SNURF... SNURF...
?

ACK! ... MR. BUN BUN HAS BEEN RUNNING AWAY A LOT, HUH?...
...HE WANTED TO TRY YOUR BED THERE.
HEE HEE

AAAAAAAAAAH...

?!
AHRF! THE BRAT!

GRUMPF!
MR. BUN BUN WAS LOOKING FOR IDEAS FOR HIS CLOTHES.
HA HA

DEDJIOUMPF...
MR. BUN BUN TOLD ME HE REALLY WANTED TO STUDY AT YOUR SCHOOL.

AGRRRR...
COME ON, MR. BUN BUN, YOU HAVE TO STOP RUNNERING LIKE THAT...

?
MAUREEN... COME QUICK AND SEE... YOU'RE GOING TO A-DORE-IT!

MR. BUN BUN WANTED TO TRY SOMETHING NEW...
AND I THINK HE LOVES CLEANING!
BZRRRRR

CAZENOVE & WILLIAM

YOU HAVE TO STOP LYING... OTHERWISE, YOUR NOSE WILL GET LONG LIKE PINOCCHIO'S.
?!
SWIPE
AND IT'LL STAY LIKE THAT!

YOUR NOSE WILL GET LONGER...
...LONGER...
...LONGER...
BIG BANG THEORY

HEE HEE
CLICK
ZAP
BRILLIANT!

MMMM... THAT SMELLS TOO GOOOOD!
SNIFF
SNIFF
SNIFF

11...12...
...18...
PONG
PONG
PONG
RECORD BROKEN!

MWAH HA... YOUR SPARROW NOSERCHIEF'S CRAZY!
MWARF ARF

YOUR STORY ABOUT PINOCCHIO'S NOSE DIDN'T IMPRESS HER, THEN?

I GOT 120 OUT OF 100 IN MATH, DADDY...
BUT THE SQUIRREL ATE MY GRADE... OTHERWISE I COULD'VE SHOWN IT TO YOU.
CLIP
CLIP
SNIP
I'D SAY SHE'S LOOKING FORWARD TO IT!

CAZENOVE & WILLIAM

HEY, WENDY. HAVE YOU LOOKED IN THE MAILBOX?
DID YOU GET A LETTER, MAYBE?
?!
ANYWAY, I'M JUST SAYING THAT. I DUNNO, EH...

SOOOO... IS THERE SOMETHING THERE FOR *YOU?*
AH, WELL, THEN, YES.

WELL, WELL, A POSTCARD WITHOUT A STAMP... BUT WHO COULD'VE SENT IT TO ME?
YOU'LL HAVE TO READ IT TO FIND OUT.

"LOADS AND LOADS OF KISSES TO MY SISTER WHO I LOVE EVEN MORE THAN A CHUNK OF CHOCOLATE!"
SIGNED, "YOUR MAUREEN WHO ADORES YOU!"

OOOH... THAT'S TOOO SWEEET... I LOVE YOU, TOO, SWEETIE!
MUAH! SMACK SMACK
HEE HEE HEE
YOU'RE TICKLING MY CHEEK...

I'M GOING TO PIN IT UP ABOVE MY BED RIGHT AWAY!
HUH?

NO, THAT WON'T WORK?!
GIVE ME THAT!
GRAB

I NEED THAT CARD TO WRITE TO MOMMY... THEN DADDY, AND ALSO LULU... AND NAT...
... EVERYTHING'S NOT JUST FOR YOU... YOU GO-IST!
ERASE ERASE RUB RUB ERASE ERASE RUB
ERASE ERASE ERASE

CAZENOVE & WILLIAM

DOUDOUS MOBIL

WE'RE ALMOST READY TO GO TO THE BEACH.
MAUREEN, DID YOU GET YOUR SUNHAT AND SUNGLASSES?
THERE MAY NOT BE A STORE THERE.
OOPS!

I'M READY! AND I BROUGHT SOME SNORKEY GEARS...
THERE WON'T BE ANY THERE...

I ALSO GRABBED THE GAME, OLD MAID.
WELL PLAYED, SISTER!

AYYY... I'VE GOT MY UNICORN FLOAT IN CASE THERE ISN'T A SEA THERE.
WE'RE WAITING JUST FOR YOU. HURRY UP!

OOPS! I ALMOST FORGOT...

IT'D BE A GOOD IDEA TO BRING WATER...
...IF THERE'RE A LOT OF PEOPLE THERE, MAYBE THERE WON'T BE ENOUGH THERE FOR US?!

CAZENOVE & WILLIAM

OH, WELL, YES. I THOUGHT MY NOSE WOULD GET LONG IF I LIED...
MY SISTER TOLD ME AND I BELIEVED EVERYTHING MY SISTER SAID!
I CAN CONFIRM THAT!
HEE HEE

DID WENDY MAKE YOU SWALLOW OTHER FIBS?
OH, MY, YES... YOU HAVE NO IDEA, MASE!

DO YOU REMEMBER, MAUREEN, WHEN I TOLD YOU THE EASTER BUNNY HAD SPILLED HIS LOAD OF CHOCOLATES IN THE WOODS?
HELLO!
HELLO HELLO... LITTLE BUNNY?
OR ALSO WHEN I TOLD YOU THAT GOBLINS MAKE THE WATER RUN WHEN YOU TURN ON THE FAUCET...
GO AHEAD, WENDY...
TURN IT ON FULL BLAST. I'M KEEPING AN EYE ON THEM!

THAT'S OKAY. LUCKILY, I GREW UP AFTER THAT.
IT'S A REAL PITY, BECAUSE I'VE GOT TONS MORE STILL.
LIKE WHAT?

WELL, THAT IT'S SQUARE COWS THAT MAKE STICKS OF BUTTER...
CRAZY!
...THAT TO ATTRACT A UNICORN, YOU HAVE TO CLAP YOUR SHOES TOGETHER AND DO A RAIN DANCE...

WIP WIP TAK TAK TAK

TAK TAK
TAK
WHEN IT COMES TO UNICORNS, MY SISTER WILL NEVER GROW UP!
TAK
HOYOOH OYOYOOH OHYOH
COME ONNNN, SHOW YOURSELVES...

CAZENOVE & WILLIAM

WATCH OUT FOR PAPERCUTZ™

elcome to the silly, somewhat superstitious, super-powered seventh THE SISTERS graphic novel, "Lucky Brat," by Christophe azenove, writer, and William Maury, co-writer and artist, from Papercutz, those perpetually rainbow-chasing do-gooders edicated to publishing great graphic novels for all ages. I'm Jim Salicrup, Editor-in-Chief and the Luckiest Man in Comics, ere with some thoughts regarding THE SISTERS and another Papercutz graphic novel or two that are sure to excite you...

ne of the many things we love about THE SISTERS is that it's set in a world that we clearly recognize—our world. Everywhere ou look in the so-called real world is filled with traces of pop culture, and that's exactly how it is in THE SISTERS! As much as I ve the *Dennis the Menace* comicstrip, it seems to be forever stuck in the '50s as the only pop culture characters Dennis seems be aware of are generic cowboys. But in THE SISTERS, it sometimes seems as if artist William has crammed every background ith as many cartoon and comics characters as possible. Many times it's very obvious, sometimes, it's a bit subtler. In THE STERS #5 "M.Y.O.B.," I don't think I would've caught one visual gag if Papercutz wasn't also publishing ASTERIX. ASTERIX, in ase you haven't heard, is one of the most successful comics characters everywhere in the world... well, almost everywhere. STERIX is still relatively unknown in the United States, and Papercutz is hoping to change that. Set in the year 50 BC, the ries is about a small village of Gauls who are resisting the mighty forces of the Roman Empire who would very much like to vade and conquer them. How is it possible for this tiny village to fend off such verwhelming forces? They've got a secret weapon—their druid has concocted magic potion that gives them all super-strength. But only two brave villagers do ost of the fighting—Asterix, "a shrewd little warrior with a keen intelligence," and s best friend Obelix, "a menhir (tall, upright, stone monuments) deliveryman, he ves eating wild boar, and getting into brawls." So, let me show you exactly what n talking about. Here's that panel from THE SISTERS #5:

nd here's Asterix's best buddy, Obelix:

I would've never given that nice lady's swimsuit a second look if I hadn't been editing hundreds of pages of ASTERIX recently. I didn't even notice her tiny Dogmatix tattoo until Papercutz designer, JayJay Jackson, pointed it out. But that's just one example. In this very graphic novel alone, you'll find hidden or right out in the open, on clothes, books, TV screens, as plush toys, or whatever, the following:

zombie (another comics series by azenove and William)
ames P. "Sulley" Sullivan (From Monsters c.)
Rabbid (Remember the Papercutz raphic novels?)
nocchio
ne Incredibles
murf (Another Papercutz crossover!)
pace Invaders
y Neighbor Totoro
hostbusters
pongeBob SquarePants (and friends)
stro Boy
weety Bird
ngry Birds
laf (and other characters from Frozen)
Mickey Mouse
The Mystery Machine (from Scooby Doo)
Captain America's shield
Pete's Dragon
Bruce Lee/Bride (from Kill Billl)
Calvin and Hobbes
Red Fraggle (from Fraggle Rock)
Bugs Bunny
Tasmanian Devil
Mr. Potato Head
Harley Quinn
Hit Girl
Badtz-Maru
Cat & Cat (Yet another Papercutz crossover!)
The Flash
Stewie Griffin (from Family Guy)
Pocahantas
Spider-Gwen/Spider-Woman/ Ghost Spider
Doc and Marty (from Back to the Future)
Baby Groot
Wallace and Gromit
Pikachu
Wonder Woman
The Incredible Hulk
Shazam/The original Captain Marvel
Peter Paprker/Spider-Man
Sonic the Hedgehog
Guns and Roses
The Big Bang Theory
Iron Maiden
Finding Nemo
Stranger Things

nd that's just the characters I could identify! Who knows who else is lurking in these pages? The point is, the stories are reat fun all by themselves, but having all these fun cameo appearances not only makes it even more fun, it also provides degree of verisimilitude.

/ell, on the following pages, everything's pretty much out in the open. It's a preview of GEEKY F@B 5 #4 "Food Fight for ona." Written by the daughter/mother team of Lucy and Liz Lareau, and illustrated by Ryan Jampole. GEEKY F@B 5 features sters Lucy and Marina Monroe, as well as friends Zara Kumar, Sofia Martinez, A.J. Jones, and Hubble the cat. Together they ackle seemingly impossible problems, but prove that when girls stick together, almost anything is possible.

s for Wendy and Maureen, they'll be back, along with a ast of thousands, in the next THE SISTERS graphic novel oming soon. If you start counting the cameo appearances this graphic novel, chances are THE SISTERS #8 will be ere before you finish counting!

nanks, JIM

STAY IN TOUCH!

EMAIL: salicrup@papercutz.com
WEB: www.papercutz.com
TWITTER: @papercutzgn
INSTAGRAM: @papercutzgn
FACEBOOK: PAPERCUTZGRAPHICNOVELS
FANMAIL: Papercutz, 160 Broadway, Suite 700, East Wing, New York, NY 10038

CHAPTER ONE: A SPARKLY BLAST

"HI, IT'S ME, LUCY MONROE! IT'S AFTER SCHOOL, AND I'M WITH MY GEEKY FAB 5 FRIENDS HEADING TO MY BESTIE, SOFIA'S HOUSE, WHERE SHE AND HER MOM, MS. MARTINEZ, ARE GETTING READY FOR AN AFTERNOON FOR US TO BAKE AND RAISE MONEY FOR EARHART ELEMENTARY'S COMPUTER LAB...
OKAY, LET'S CHECK OUR INGREDIENTS BEFORE YOUR FRIENDS COME OVER TO HELP...
FLOUR... CHECK. SUGAR... CHECK. BUTTER... BAKING SODA... CHECK, CHECK. FOOD COLORING... CHECK.
FOOD COLORING? WHAT KIND OF CAKE IS THIS?
IT'S A RAINBOW CAKE, MOM. WE NEED LOTS OF COLOR FOR A RAINBOW CAKE... AND GLITTER!
HUG THE COOK
RED
BLUE
GREEN
YELLOW
FLOUR
RAW SUGAR
GLITTER? YOU CAN'T EAT GLITTER!
HUG THE COOK
YES, YOU CAN. WE ARE GOING TO MAKE IT WITH THIS RAW SUGAR AND FOOD COLORING.
HMMM...I'M GOING TO HAVE TO CHECK THAT OUT...
SOFIA
IT'S SUPER EASY AND WE CAN MAKE ALL COLORS OF THE RAINBOW! I SAW IT ON YOUTUBE!
DING DONG
UH-OH! IT'S A GEEKY FAB 5 KITCHEN INVASION!
HUG THE COOK
SOFIA

SOFIA
HEY, EVERYONE! READY TO BAKE A RAINBOW?
YES!
SOUNDS LIKE A PLAN: YOU MAKE IT. I'LL EAT IT. MMM

I MADE YOU EACH A SURPRISE! YOU KNOW HOW I LOVE TO DESIGN AND SEW CLOTHES... SO...

FOR YOU ZARA, THE MUSICAL MATH WHIZ... A SPECIAL APRON...
I LOVE IT!

FOR OUR FUTURE MARTIAN ASTRONAUT, MARINA...
OH, MY STARS!
FOR A.J., OUR FUTURE ENGINEER...
COOL! THERE'S EVEN A LOOP FOR MY HAMMER...
CHEF AT WORK
FOR LUCY, WHO WANTS TO SAVE OUR PLANET, AND JUST ABOUT EVERYTHING AND EVERYONE...
SAVE OUR OCEANS! BAN PLASTIC STRAWS!
AND FOR HUBBLE... YOU ARE OFFICIALLY OUR CAT IN THE CHEF HAT!
YEAH, CHEF. SUUURE. JUST WAIT UNTIL I ADD IN MY SECRET INGREDIENT... MOUSE CRÈME.

Don't miss GEEKY F@B 5 #4 "Food Fight for Fiona" available now from booksellers an libraries everywhere.